*The Elfdins
and the
Gold Temple*

The Elfdins and the Gold Temple

An Oralee Chronicle

R. C. Jette

RESOURCE *Publications* • Eugene, Oregon

Resource Publications
An Imprint of Wipf and Stock Publishers
199 W. 8th Ave., Suite 3
Eugene, OR 97401

www.wipfandstock.com

PAPERBACK ISBN: 978-1-5326-6462-5
HARDCOVER ISBN: 978-1-5326-6463-2
EBOOK ISBN: 978-1-5326-6464-9

Manufactured in the U.S.A.   OCTOBER 10, 2018

This book is dedicated to my Lord who makes all things possible by faith and to my husband, my children and my grandchildren.

He delivered me from my strong enemy, and from them which hated me: for they were too strong for me (Psalms 18:17, KJV).

Contents

Prelude

CLOAKED WITH AN EERIE veil of foreboding, the Sovereign God's glory is hidden to the Elfdins of Oralee. These Elvin beings no longer live in affluence in the Gold Valley, but dwell in stone huts on Gold Mountain inside the circumference of the gold crosses.

During Oralee's Golden Age, Human worshippers of the Sovereign God entered through the Portal in the Gold Temple. But since the Krog invasion, the Dins, nickname of the Elfdins, have never seen a Human and most have never travelled beyond the circumference of the gold crosses.

Members of the Warband, warriors skilled in the art of archery and defense, are the only ones to leave the boundary of the crosses. In order to hunt for food, they must travel into the Ravine that is before the Great Forest that leads to Gold Valley. This is terrifying to a people who once possessed supernatural power given to them by the Sovereign God.

In fact, until the Krogs, there was no need to live in huts within the circumference of the crosses, to have a Warband or to have knowledge of defensive weaponry. Oralee was a paradise of peace and prosperity without evil for not only the Elfdins, but for their Human visitors.

Prologue

SPIRITUAL MENTOR GILBERT RHYS was unaware that a figure cloaked in black, hiding in the shadows, watched him as he went about his business. After the last Human went back through the Portal, he made sure the Gold Cross, imprinted with the words *Sovereign God* that blocked the Portal, faced Oralee. He then walked to the temple doors, did a mental check of the interior, and closed the huge doors. Once outside, he hurried to the Gold Valley and its gold castles to find the others waiting for him. It was time for all Elfdins to make their yearly trek to the gold crosses on Gold Mountain to celebrate their Great Festival. This was the time of great rejoicing for the bountiful harvest given to them by the Sovereign God.

All the Dins gathered inside the gold crosses and faced the platform that stood in front of the largest cross. On the platform, Gilbert and his wife Rowena sat next to High Prince Cadwy and High Princess Heidi. With anticipation rising, there was not a whisper heard as all watched the Great Prophet Arthur Dewey and Great Prophetess Guinevere raise their arms to invoke the Sovereign God's blessing.

With the invocation, the people began to sing, "*Sovereign God, we worship you. Sovereign God, we worship you. We praise you our God. We praise you our God.*" But Gilbert was distracted by movement in the tall grass beyond the crosses. He went to investigate with the belief that a bairn, or young Din, had strayed from its Ma and Pa. But he wasn't prepared for the black, long-haired beast with sinister eyes that he encountered. Never had he seen anything like it in all his years. Although he was one of the most powerful of the Dins, he was on his back before he could react. The beast had both Gilbert's arms pinned by huge claws and its teeth were piercing into his chest.

Gilbert being stunned from the impact couldn't move. But apparently his dilemma had been seen. For in seconds, Arthur, Guinevere, and Rowena ran in his direction with Cadwy and several ancestrals close behind. In a flash, the great prophet gave a forward motion of both hands that sent bolts of lightning and knocked the thing off Gilbert. Right after Arthur's bolt, Rowena's followed and completely stunned the beast. With that, Guinevere raised her hands and followed with a ball of fire that consumed the beast in flames.

Cadwy and some of the ancestrals carried Gilbert back to the platform to have his wounds healed by Guinevere. In a matter of minutes, he was healed. As he got up, he noticed more of the hideous things outside the gold crosses, but not a one moved to enter inside. When he sent a ball of fire at them, he saw what looked like a Din dressed in black wave his arm. That motion caused Gilbert's ball of fire to bounce off some sort of shield. Arthur, Guinevere, Rowena, Cadwy, and Heidi tried to penetrate it, but failed. Then the entire Dins' power together couldn't breach the shield.

At that time, Arthur decreed that all Dins remain inside the boundary of the gold crosses. They were to build stone huts with thatched roofs as temporary dwellings, until they knew what evil possessed more power than the great prophet, the great prophetess, the spiritual mentors, the high prince, and the high princess. Gilbert tried to get Arthur to change his mind, and even suggested that he and Cadwy travel back to the Gold Temple and get the Humans to help. But Arthur would hear none of it.

Although the great prophet never said why, Gilbert knew what he thought. If the spiritual mentors, who are not only their spiritual instructors, but the ones who transmitted the supernatural power through the laying on of their hands, could be overtaken by such a beast, what of the bairns who had no supernatural power until the spiritual mentors laid hands on them when they turned twelve?

But that decision placed the Elfdins of Oralee in their present four hundred years of Dark Age. In their ignorance, they started the use of physical warfare instead of supernatural and were placed far away from the Gold Temple and all their Sacred Books.

Chapter 1

The Awakening Begins

GRIFFIN ALUN WATCHED THE others around him. Tonight the Warband needed to replenish the food storage for the colony. But his mind wandered from his purpose. He sensed something different in the Ravine around Gold Mountain. It was a feeling that he couldn't name. It felt like the beginning or the ending. Of what, he had no understanding. His skin crawled more than usual under the dreary shroud. But as the future great prophet, he didn't want to alarm the others.Besides, lately, there were a lot of things that he didn't understand.

"What's up?" David asked placing his right hand on Griffin's left shoulder.

Griffin knew he'd better be tactful, because how their future high prince reacted to his response would influence the others. "Just feel a little tired." It was obvious by David's scrunched eyebrows that he questioned the answer. But Griffin was grateful when David turned and beckoned the others to continue the hunt.

It was Squire Owen that gave the shout of danger and pointed to Griffin's left. "Krog!"

Griffin turned, but the beast was on top of him before anyone could discharge an arrow. As he felt its claws dig into his chest and warm liquid ooze out, he thought it was all over for him. When he gained consciousness, he was on a stretcher carried by some of the Warband. He heard David order everyone to hurry back to the colony and Griffin sensed distress in his voice. "David!" He said. "I'm okay."

David's eyes bulged. "Are you sure?"

"Quite sure," he said, trying to sit up.

David stopped him. "Your wounds need tending." He put up his hands. "No disrespect meant. But when we pushed that beast off, you didn't look too healthy."

Griffin felt that strangeness again and caught David's puzzled gaze. Maybe he should say something. "I keep wondering what Oralee was like without Krogs."

David rubbed the back of his neck with his right hand. "Don't we all."

"I feel it's time to do something more than just stating what we want."

David laughed. "I think that Krog has addled your brain."

Griffin pulled David's forest green tunic with his right hand. "I'm serious. You know that I don't jest."

Bringing back the old days troubled more than Griffin; there were others beginning to battle the same desire. For back at the colony, fifteen-year-old Catrin Ryn's mind craved the return of the Golden Age. She tried to control her desire by working hard at her weapons and defense tactics. But Meghan's acceptance of their lot infuriated her, and made her more determined to succeed.She was thankful for her sister Rhonda, who was similar to herself in many ways. However, their brother David seemed to distant himself from them; this infuriated Catrin who felt that she was as much a warrior as the boys. Besides, as the next great prophetess, she was three foot six inches. David being in line to be the next high prince was only three foot four inches. Since the great prophet and great prophetess are the tallest, she felt that height had to be significant.

Catrin knew that she was an equal warrior with the boys. That included her brother David or Meghan's brother Griffin or any of the boys, and she wasn't going to embrace anything less. But it was unbearable being a girl in Oralee, when only male warriors were allowed to hunt.Since her Pa's sister, Arwyn Rhys, the spiritual mentor, was killed by a Krog when her lad Owen was only eight, female warriors are no longer allowed to hunt. If they had the old days back, Great Prophet Drew and Great Prophetess Meredith would be the two most powerful Dins. Since she and Griffin would fill those positions in the future, they would be almost as powerful. But until she could find a way to prove herself and bring those days back, she would have to bide her time.

She tried to get Meghan more involved with her mission. But Meghan always found some excuse for her lack of initiative. Maybe she should mention something to Griffin and her brother in the Great Hall after the hunt. Surely, they couldn't be content with the way things were, even for boys.

When she, Rhonda, and Meghan entered the Great Hall, the sight of Mistress Meredith, the great prophetess tending Griffin boggled her. "What's wrong?" She said, as she, Rhonda, and Meghan hurried towards them.

David grabbed her arm to stop her. A Krog got him, but . . ."

"It was utterly ghastly!" Owen interrupted, while nodding towards Rhonda.

"What!" Catrin gasped.

"Don't listen to him," David said, holding her arm. "Griffin is fine."

Catrin pulled her arm loose and pointed her right hand toward Griffin. "Why is Great Prophetess Meredith over him?"

"To make sure the wounds are cleaned and wrapped. She may not have the Din's supernatural power, but she is quite skillful with herbs and natural remedies."

"Catrin!" Griffin called. "Why don't you and Rhonda wait with Meghan at our hut?"

David rubbed the back of his neck. "That sounds like a good idea."

Catrin glared at her brother. "I'll go, but you know I don't like it."

Rhonda gave a loud sigh. "Certainly, let's get the weaker gender elsewhere."

"It's best we leave," Meghan said, twisting her hands.

Catrin burst out of the hall and huffed all the way to great prophet's house with Rhonda by her side as Meghan hurried behind. They no sooner entered the hut, when Meghan began her habitual surrender. She gestured towards the chairs at the table. "Please take a seat, while I get us a cup of herbal tea."

Catrin felt her stomach tense and shook both fists. "This is serious! How can you be so calm?"

"Really Catrin," Meghan said, pouring the tea. "I don't understand your fuss."

Before Catrin could answer, Rhonda sat back in the chair and folded her arms. "Essentially Meghan, when are you going to act like a warrior instead of a wimp?"

Catrin threw up her arms and walked over to the window. How she hated being treated like a girl, when she had the title of warrior just like the boys. "One of these days!" She shouted, as Meghan shot upright from her seat. "I'll show them what a warrior I am."

"Bless me!" Meghan said, holding her chest with both hands. "I have no desire to fight Krogs. It's no place for females. I thought you would agree with that after Spiritual Mentor Arwyn was killed by one of those beasts. I mean, seriously Catrin. Spiritual Mentor Dylan is without a wife, and Owen is without a Ma."

Before Catrin could reply, she heard the boys enter the hut. "I feel silly being carried on this stretcher," Griffin said.

David and Owen placed the stretcher down and helped Griffin onto the sofa. David gestured with his right hand. "Whether you feel silly is not important. You need to rest. Those wounds could have been fatal."

"Ouch!" Griffin said, as he went to lie down. "I guess it does hurt."

Owen gestured with both hands. "You received some reprehensible injuries."

Meghan hurried over to fluff Griffin's pillow. "And you, my stubborn brother, will need time to heal."

Owen kicked the ground with his left foot. "If I had the power the spiritual mentor's renowned for, I'd have used phenomenal supernatural power against the beast."

Rhonda jumped out of her chair. "Outstanding!"

Griffin reached for Owen's hand. "If I had, is something that we can all say."

"Fair enough," Owen answered. "But you must acknowledge that when the spiritual mentor, my Pa, laid hands on us when we became squires at twelve, we were all eager to be endowed with supernatural power."

Rhonda fidgeted with her left earlobe. "I completely concur."

Catrin felt this was the time to mention the old days. "What we need to do is bring back the Golden Age. Then we . . ."

"Indeed!" Griffin interrupted while shrieking in Pain. "That's what I was telling David on our way back from the hunt."

"Not this again," Meghan said, rolling her eyes. "You'll all frazzle your brain with ways to bring back the old days."

"Better frazzled than apathetic," Owen said.

Rhonda nodded to Owen. "You are so accurate. I cannot fathom how any intelligent Din can be satisfied with such ludicrous indifference?"

Catrin threw up her arms. "Besides, I would like to know how any Din can desire this nothing life."

Griffin made a tent with his fingers and tapped his lips with his forefingers. "That is what I would like to know."

"My mental faculty has been reflecting the same contemplation," Owen said.

Catrin gestured with both hands. "Thinking doesn't get us anywhere. We need to do something."

Rhonda shook both fists. "Precisely, deliberation will not annihilate Krogs from Oralee nor will it reinstate our supernatural power."

David folded his arms and shook his head. "We can talk all we want, but it's up to the high prince and warlord of the Elfdins to say what's to be done."

Catrin clenched her right fist. "In the old days, the great prophet and great prophetess led the people with commanding supernatural power; they were the leaders of the Dins before the Krogs stole our supernatural power." She let out a heavy sigh. "Now, both of them are powerless and so are we."

Griffin's face whitened. "You know it's not my Pa's fault."

Meghan nodded her head. "Pa marrying our Ma who is the sister of your Pa, the high prince, corrected the lineage."

"And don't forget," Griffin said, "the correct bloodline is the rule set down by the Sovereign God. And he made clear who was to marry who by our physical appearance. All prophets and prophetesses are three foot six with raven black hair and emerald green eyes, all spiritual mentors are three foot five with ash blond hair and gray eyes, and all prince and princesses are three foot four with blond hair and sapphire blue eyes. That leaves no question as to who is to marry who." He tapped his lips with his right forefinger. "But all that aside, my Pa and I don't believe that the Krogs stole our supernatural power. We believe that if Arthur Dewey's grand lad hadn't started the great prophet's marrying outside of the high prince's family and the required physical requirements, we'd still have our supernatural power."

"I meant no offense to you or your Pa." Catrin clenched both fists. "It's just that we do nothing, and let the Krogs destroy us."

"Not only that," Rhonda interjected, "they've kept us imprisoned on this mountain for centuries. Because of that, we have no comprehension if anything from the Golden Age exists. It is all so wretched that our ancestors acquiesced to the confinement."

"Revelation!" Owen said, jumping to his feet. "That's it, now I know why my Pa is not a real spiritual mentor, and because of that he still feels responsible for my Ma's fatality."

David's eyebrows scrunched together. "What in Oralee are you talking about?"

"With the erroneous ancestry in the great prophet it disturbed the stability." Owen whacked his head with his left hand. "Why didn't I perceive that previous?"

David threw up both hands. "Wait a minute! What does that have to do with you? You're Ma was my Pa's sister. There's no wrong ancestry."

Griffin slowly sat up. "I do believe he's got it right. Yes, his Ma had the correct ancestry. But because the great prophet and great prophetess are supposed to be the spiritual leaders, the balance of power has been unsettled."

Catrin gestured with both hands. "Excuse me, but if the correct ancestry has been fixed with you, Meghan, and Vanora's Ma being our Pa's sister, where's our supernatural power? Last time I checked, we seem to be powerless."

"Exceptional, Catrin." Rhonda said matter-of-factly.

Meghan twisted her hands and looked down. "That's the first sensible thing I've heard."

"I believe," Griffin said, scratching the back of his head with his right hand, "that we need to see if there are still Humans here."

"Now you're talking!" Catrin said, punching the air with her right fist.

Rhonda did a two-step. "This is getting remarkable! I believe that the necessity for us to reclaim our supernatural power has been ignored far too long."

Meghan's eyes widened. "I can't be hearing this right. The only way that we can find out if there are Humans is to travel beyond the Ravine at the bottom of Gold Mountain?"

"Precisely!" Owen said.

"Wait a minute!" David said. "How many times do I have to say this? It's not up to us; we do not make decisions for this colony. High Prince Patrick, who is our warlord, has to do it, and he will not do anything without conferring with our Ma, High Princess Winifred."

Meghan twisted her hands. "Besides, we don't have any idea what lies beyond the Ravine." Her eyes bulged. "It could be more dangerous than just Krogs."

Catrin felt her blood boil. "Something must be done! Someone has to get our supernatural power back."

David paced back and forth, as if fighting his emotions. "But what can we do?"

"We could supplicate the Sovereign God," Owen said.

Rhonda clapped her hands. "Owen, you are magnificent."

Catrin placed her hands on her hips. "And how do we do that?"

David rubbed the back of his neck with his right hand. "We don't even know if he still exists."

Owen combed his ash blond hair back with his fingers. "I can't fathom him annihilating himself."

Rhonda shot her left fist into the air. "That's precisely my assessment."

"First of all," Griffin said, "working ourselves into a dither won't help our thoughts." He patted his lips with his right forefinger. "But maybe we could help our parents decide to do something?"

Catrin punched the air with her right fist. "That's it!"

Rhonda and Owen both did a little jig and said in unison. "Exceptional!"

Meghan's mouth dropped. "Dear me! What are you all saying?"

Catrin twirled her raven black hair around her right forefinger. "Maybe I can plead with my Pa to do something."

Griffin smiled. "I knew you'd get it, and I'll bring the subject up to my Pa. After all, the great prophet should have some answers."

Owen shrugged his shoulders. "And I'll converse with my Pa. He may be spiritually impotent, but he is supposed to be the spiritual mentor."

Rhonda laughed. "I'll just stay out of the way for this one. If anything goes afoul, maybe I can facilitate reconciliation. After all, as the future spiritual mentor, I should be able to help resolve disagreements."

David folded his arms and shook his head. "I hope we're not set for trouble. But something has to be done. We just can't continue to do nothing, or we'll become extinct."

Griffin sighed. "Now, all we have to do is to convince High Prince Patrick, High Princess Winifred, Great Prophet Drew, Great Prophetess Meredith, and Spiritual Mentor Dylan to recognize the dilemma." He paused and looked toward David and Rhonda. "I meant no offense to you two, but you both do understand why it is wiser that Catrin and I lay the foundation. Your Pa seems to respect her judgment. I believe it is because she will be the next great prophetess. Equally, my Pa seems to respect my judgment. I believe it is because he finally corrected the ancestry in the future great prophet. Both of our Pas know that the spiritual leaders of the Dins have always had the superior role."

David laughed. "No problem there. Future role or not, I know Catrin's ways, but I don't dare try them. They seem cute to Pa coming from her, but from me . . ." He Paused. "Well, let's just say that I'll stand on the sideline for this one and wait until he asks for me."

Rhonda fidgeted with her left earlobe. "I found it easier to let Catrin take the lead. After all, she is in line to be the next great prophetess."

Meghan twisted her hands. "I guess I'll stay out of it too. In our house, it's my brother who seems to have a way with both parents. I think they think that I'm too fearful." She shuffled her feet and looked down. "But I must go on record as warning of its danger."

The others all laughed in unison. "It's recorded."

Chapter 2

The Ballad

CATRIN WAITED UNTIL THE high prince was alone before she approached the subject. "Pa," she pouted.

"What is it, sweetie?" He tapped his legs with his hands. "Tell your Pa all about it."

She sat on his lap and looked into his eyes. "Have you ever wished to celebrate the Great Festival and to use supernatural power?"

He ran his fingers along the scar from his right temple to his chin. "I must admit that I've thought of it many times."

"If we only knew what happened to the Humans." Her emerald eyes filled with tears. "Our people were never sickly. Now," she sobbed, "we die before our time. If we had our supernatural power, your sister Arwyn would still be alive. It's just ghastly that Owen has no Ma and Dylan is still grieving." She wiped her eyes. "Can't something be done to deliver our land from the beasts?"

"There, there, my dear, you're in a dither." He gave out a heavy sigh. "But I do wish I could rid Oralee of the beasts. I dearly miss Arwyn." He paused, and his eyebrows scrunched together. "Wait a minute! When I was a bairn, my great-ancestral-ma told me about a Portal that her ancestral-ma told her existed between the Humans and Oralee at the Gold Temple."

"There's a Portal between the two worlds?" Catrin said as she jumped off his lap.

"Yes, but we'd have to find the Gold Temple first."

"How will the Portal help?"

"Only Humans could destroy the Krogs from our land. Believe me, when I tell you that we're no match against those evil beasts. Their hatred is so severe against us. Every time that we manage to slay one, there's two in its place. Besides," he said, tracing the scar from his right temple to his chin, "we have no idea how many there are; there could be thousands for all we know."

Catrin figured that she'd concentrate on talking about Humans and not Krogs. "Are Humans that big?"

"It's not their size. Well, I mean, they can be about six feet tall. But it is their supernatural power."

Catrin's face screwed up. "What do you mean? I thought Dins were just as powerful?"

"No Din ever had the power to leave Oralee, but the Humans entered in and out through that Portal."

"Wow!" She said, punching the air with her right fist. "We need to find the Humans."

Patrick folded his arms and sat back in his chair. "We don't even know if there are any Humans at the Gold Temple. Surely, they would have come to the Gold Mountain by now."

Catrin placed her hands on her hips. "Maybe they left records at the temple."

Patrick rubbed his forehead with his hands. "But I don't know its location, or if the Krogs inhabit it. Without knowledge of its whereabouts, I could find myself at the opposite end of Oralee." He lowered his voice to a whisper. "Too much is at stake. We've lost too many to Krogs already." He shook his head and gave a heavy sigh, as he stood up. "Arwyn would still be here if we had kept females from joining the hunt."

Catrin's stomach knotted. "So, would a lot of the male warriors still be here, if they hadn't gone on the hunt. I know she was your sister, but how many have lost Pas, brothers, husbands, etc.? It's time to stop all the killing."

Patrick rubbed the scar from his right temple to his chin, "I know you're right. I just felt that it's harder for bairns to be without their Ma; she's the one that does all their training until they become squires."

Catrin felt that she had to get through to her Pa. "But surely someone in Oralee must know something about the Golden Age and the Humans?"

"I wish I knew who." He stood, cupped her face and kissed her forehead. "You deserve to experience the real Oralee." His eyes took on a haunted look. "We all need to relish the Golden Days." He began to pace the floor, rubbing his forehead with both hands. After a while, he clapped his hands and said. "The ancestrals!" He placed his right hand on Catrin's left shoulder. "Maybe some of them might have heard the ballads sung during the glorious days by one of their great-ancestrals."

She hit the air with her right fist. "Of course! That has to be it. Someone must have heard something."

"Have Herald Roth call an emergency meeting of all ancestrals to the Great Hall."

"Yes sir!" She said, her feet barely hitting the ground as she ran to deliver her message. Her mind raced with excitement. Maybe this was the beginning of their liberation from Krogs.

Catrin hid behind the great prophet's veil that separated his family's sitting area from the main hall and watched the ancestrals gather. For hours, she heard poem after poem and ballad after ballad recited without any mention of the Gold Temple or the Humans.

She watched as her Pa dismissed the assembly, drop into his seat at the great table, and droop his chin in his hands. After a few minutes, she pretended to have just entered the hall and touched his right shoulder. "Pa! What's wrong? Are you well?"

He looked up, his face bleak with disappointment. "Not a one could recall an old ballad about the Gold Temple or the Humans."

She sat next to him. "Don't we have anything about the Golden Days?"

"I believe that my ancestral-ma said something about there being Sacred Books where we could find out about everything, but I wouldn't know where to find them." He gave a helpless gesture with his hands. "Since the Krogs, we haven't been beyond the Ravine at the bottom of Gold Mountain. Everything is lost to us."

Catrin grabbed her head with both hands. "Wait a minute! I remember where I heard about the Sovereign God, the Gold Temple, and the Humans."

"What did you say?"

"I remember where I heard about the Sovereign God, the Gold Temple, and the Humans."

"But where? How?"

Before I was a squire, I used to love to watch the old Archer Rhett Howell. He sang a ballad while he practiced shooting his arrows."

High Prince Patrick's eyes widened. "Do you remember it?"

"No, but I believe that Archer might."

"Archer? W-why would he remember?"

Catrin gestured with both hands. "It was his Pa who sang it day in and day out."

"Of course!" He said. "I think all this has addled my brain." He stood up and clasped his hands together. "That's it! Go get Archer."

Catrin began to feel like Herald Roth. But she didn't mind if it meant that the Golden Age would return. When she arrived at her destination, she was relieved to find Archer and Vanora at home. With a quick apology for interrupting their dinner, she explained her mission.

Archer sat back, closed his eyes and muttered to himself. Then he jumped up, grabbed a quill and parchment.

Catrin clenched both hands against her heart as she felt it bang against her ribs. "Do you remember it?"

He laughed. "I would hope so." He gestured with his right hand. After all, my Pa sang it as if the words were supernatural. It was passed down from his great-great-ancestral-pa who repeated it continuously. I believe that my Pa thought that it would bring back the days when Dins walked with Humans."

Catrin jumped up and punched the air with her right fist. "This is great!"

He began to write. "Just give me a few moments to jot it down for you."

Catrin's stomach flipped. "I can't wait till the high prince hears this."

He handed her the parchment. "That should do it."

She pulled her hands back. "No!" She closed her eyes and took a deep breath. "I don't mean to be impolite, but you misunderstood me. High Prince Patrick wants you to go to the hall."

Catrin waited for Archer to kiss his wife. "Perhaps you shouldn't wait up for him. If he has anything that can help my Pa, it could be a long night."

Vanora yawned into her right hand. "I think you're right. It's been a long day. I think this bairn has kicked my insides black and blue." She laughed and held her stomach. "I'm sure we're going to have a great warrior like its Pa." She gave a wave with her right hand. "But you two better hurry. I do believe that we've kept the high prince waiting long enough."

Catrin and Archer hurried to the Great Hall. "My high prince," Archer said, bowing his head.

"Do you remember it?" Patrick sounded anxious. He paused, took a deep breath, and grinned at his daughter. "I guess I sound a little impatient, but Catrin has me anxious about the Golden Age."

Archer handed him the parchment with the words of the ballad. "I don't understand it, but it's obviously something about the Gold Temple and Humans." His eyes saddened. "My Pa sang it, like some supernatural call while he shot arrows at the target."

Patrick took the ballad and read the words out loud.

> "The sun sleeps at night,
> It rises at dawn,
> Follow the daytime,

Quest a fortnight long.
At the Gold Temple,
Observe the Gold Cross,
Touch the carved Pundle,
Greet past Humans."

Catrin listened with strained nerves. "Does it help?"

"I think," Archer interjected, "that my Pa thought it would bring back the old days and rid Oralee of Krogs."

Patrick starred at the words. "Wow!" This is a bit much for me. I believe that we had better call in your in-laws, Great Prophet Drew and Great Prophetess Meredith, and their lad Griffin." He rubbed his temple with his right hand. "I don't know how much help Meghan will be, but she is the future high princess. Anyway, let's hope that they can interpret this ballad." He turned towards Catrin. "You'll need to get Spiritual Mentor Dylan, your Ma, and brother to come also."

"Okay, but I don't think that you are going to be able to leave squires Rhonda and Owen out. After all, they are the future spiritual mentors," she said, throwing up her arms.

Patrick laughed. "You might be right, but they will have to be quiet. I know that will be difficult for those two, but I want to hear from their elders at this time." He gestured with his right hand. "Make sure that they know that I want them out of this. If I ask for their help, they may respond. Otherwise, they are to remain quiet."

Catrin laughed. "I'm sure that they will obey. After all, the fact that they are in their first official gathering of the elders will have them both quite excited.

Chapter 3

The Root of Oralee's Evil

EVIL DRUXIN SAT IN the Great Ancestral Cave that housed the stone coffins of the ancestrals. He perused the Sacred Books of the Dins lined up on wooden shelves. After the Dins were imprisoned on Gold Mountain, he stole the books and the shelves from the Gold Temple.

He grinned, leaned back in his chair, and crossed his arms. "Maybe I should destroy all these ancient writings, especially the Holy Bibles that speak of him. But then again, I like having them around." Raven, the eldest of the Krogs, curled up the left side of his mouth. Evil patted his head. "You know me so well," he snickered. "It's a constant reminder of my cunning that will annihilate any trace of worship to the Sovereign God." He clasped his hands with long fingernails that almost pierced his flesh and looked up. "Well, you're not so superior any more. Very shortly, I shall be the only god the Dins will know." He pointed his right forefinger toward Heaven. "What did you gain by choosing Arthur, my twin brother, to be great prophet? He's dead and I'm over four hundred years old with power to live for thousands of years. I don't care that he fit the physical requirements, I was the firstborn. You could have made me three foot six inches with raven black hair and emerald green eyes like any other prophet and prophetess. Instead, you made me a naught at three feet with brown hair and brown eyes. But as soon as I became proficient enough in my black power, I changed my hair to black and my eyes to emerald green." Druxin gave an evil grin. "Let me tell you that I'm about to be the ultimate of all great prophets. Once I'm ready to go to the Gold Temple, I'll destroy the Gold Cross and prevent any Humans from entering Oralee ever again. Then, I shall transform myself into the perfect great prophet and fool all the Elfdins into thinking that I am the Sovereign God. It's you who is about to become naught."

He sat back and stared towards the fireplace. With a move of his right hand, a pot lifted off the hearth, poured its liquid into a mug on the nearby table, and set itself back on the hearth. Then with another move of his right hand, the cup glided across the room to his hand. He took a sip and placed the cup on the table beside his chair. Then with a move of his right hand towards the mantle, his pipe and tobacco were instantly in his hand. He gave a deep laugh and looked up. "Your favorites were so gullible; they actually believed that they had no power against my shield. I deceived them into believing that they were powerless. Not a one was able to see the hundreds of Krogs that they had killed that day. Now the fools use physical warfare." He gave a low sneer. "Even my stupid brother was deceived; he imprisoned them all on that mountain." He ran his fingernails through his black beard. "It's almost time for me to have my revenge on you and Oralee."

Raven jumped up on the nearby table, picked up a gold cross on a gold chain with his teeth and dropped it into Evil Druxin's lap. Evil picked it up, held it in his hand, and felt his confidence spiral upward. "Well, Sovereign God, poor Sir Reginald's cross did him no good. He's dead and I have his gold cross." He laughed. "I can assure you that you are going to lose this time." His voice raised an octave. "I can't find any faithful followers. They don't even know who you are; you're a thing of the past. Just like I promised." He lit his pipe, sat back, and closed his eyes. "I'll not rest till all your favorites are destroyed, and Oralee has no remembrance that you ever existed."

Before Evil finished his tea, it was time for the elder Krogs to assemble at the cave. With a wave of his right hand, the door opened to let Carbon, Nightshade, and Soot in. He gave a wicked grin as they purred with anticipation. "It won't be long, my pets," he said. "Things are going as expected. It's almost time for us to head for the Gold Temple and finish my revenge."

Evil chortled as Raven hissed and swat the air. "You can taste the sweet revenge." He cupped his hands. "The Sovereign God won't stop us. I'll become great prophet and destroy all signs of worship to anything but myself." His sinister laugh rang through the nighttime.

Once Catrin returned to the Great Hall with the others, Patrick noticed that Winifred wasn't there. "Where's your Ma?"

Catrin threw up her arms. "You know Ma. She wanted to let all of the other leaders see what is what first. If she can be of help after, she will. I tried to talk her into coming, but she felt that getting tomorrow's cooking done was more helpful at present."

Patrick folded his arms and chuckled. "I should have known. Your Ma has never liked taking part in anything before Drew, Meredith, Dylan, and I have a say." He hung his head. "Of course that used to include Arwyn." He shook his head, took a deep breath, and exhaled. Then he ushered Great Prophet Drew, Great Prophetess Meredith, and Spiritual Mentor Dylan to all gather at his family table to decipher the words of the ballad, while Griffin, David, Catrin, and Meaghan sat nearby. Owen and Rhonda watched and listened from a distant table.

They'd spent hours reciting the ballad over and over again without any headway.

Drew's eyebrows squished together. "This is a tough one."

Meredith stood up and stretched her arms up. "I've never heard the likes."

Patrick sat back and folded his arms. "I must admit, it has me quite addled."

"Likewise, it's exclusively complex," Dylan said, throwing up his arms.

David got up from his chair and paced back and forth. "But it must be deciphered, or we'll never get rid of the Krogs."

Patrick stood up, walked over to David, and placed his right hand on his left shoulder. "Listen lad, we're all as anxious as you to figure this out, but we must calm down. Getting in a dither will not help."

Catrin threw her arms up. "We must be missing something. Old Archer Rhett Howell believed that it was something important. All of us are supposed to be the most powerful of the Elfdins. Surely, we are overlooking something."

"May I interject my thoughts?" Griffin asked, scratching the back of his head with his right hand.

"Of course." Patrick said, rubbing the scar from his right temple to his chin. "I believe that we could use any enlightenment at this time."

"Although we no longer see the sun, we know that it slept at nighttime in the west and rose at daytime in the east." He paused and patted his lip with his right forefinger. "That is correct, right?"

Everyone nodded.

"Well, the daytime has to mean the east to west direction of the sun. Thus, whoever goes will travel fourteen days from an east to west direction and sleep at nighttime."

Dylan jumped with excitement. "Brilliant!"

Catrin shot her right fist into the air. "That has to be it."

David clasped his hands together. "I think Griffin's got it."

Meghan twisted her hands. "Do you mean travelling beyond the Ravine?"

Rhonda and Owen came running over to the others and said in unison. "Absolutely!"

Patrick sat back down, folded his arms, and blew out a deep sigh. "What about the other half of the ballad?"

Dylan screwed up his face. "What in Oralee is a carved Pundle?"

Meredith threw up her hands. "I'd like to know what a past Human means."

Griffin tented his fingers and tapped his lips with his forefingers. "I just have this strong notion that the other half will be revealed when we find the Gold Temple."

Patrick rubbed his right temple. "Such a dangerous crusade has never been attempted. I'd have to take most of the Warband with me. That would leave the colony without protection, and I don't even want to think of that."

David rubbed the back of his neck with his right hand. "But wouldn't a multitude of Dins be easily spotted by Krogs?"

Dylan stroked his chin with the fingers of his right hand. "Perhaps a few camouflaged warriors would have a healthier possibility."

Meredith clasped her hands. "I do believe that David and Dylan have it right. It would be much easier for a few warriors to slip through than it would be for hundreds."

Patrick laughed and turned his attention toward David. "Either way, my immediate concern is telling your Ma. Although she said that she would let us all see what we thought about the ballad before she got involved, I don't know how I'm supposed to tell her that we went beyond thought to decision."

"I'll come along as backup and just nod in agreement with you." David gestured with his right hand. "Ma has always accepted truth."

"What in Oralee are you saying?" Winifred said, as she dropped her ladle. "You can't travel to the Gold Temple. No Din has left the Ravine since the invasion. Even if you took the whole Warband, it would be too dangerous. There would be too many chances for traps. Everyone would become a feast for the Krogs, and with the colony unguarded, we would all be next."

Patrick folded his arms; he'd made up his mind. "But unless we find out how to reach the Humans and get our supernatural power back, we're all doomed sooner or later."

"Besides," David said, "nothing has been done for too long. Ma, you must see that."

"I know that!" She paused, biting her bottom lip. "But can't we find an alternative?"

Patrick rubbed his right temple. "I've searched and searched my mind for options. There are none. It's time to stop thinking and take action; it's vital that we take Oralee back from the evil that hates us." He ran his fingers down the scar from his right temple to his chin. "I've decided to call those of us who undertake this quest, the Crusaders. The members of the crusade will be your brother, Warrior Gwent Alun, Spiritual Mentor Dylan Rhys, along with Warrior Archer Rhett, Warrior Fletcher Prichard, Warrior Falconer Hopper, and a couple of squires to help with carrying. That way, the warriors can remain on alert."

Winifred's eyebrows scrunched together. "Why so few?"

David gestured with his right hand. "They'll have a better chance of camouflaging themselves. A few will be able to hide more easily than a multitude."

Patrick nodded. "A few of us should have a better chance of slipping through the Krogs. I've left David in charge of the colony while I'm gone. That's not resting to well with him, but that is my decision for the benefit of the colony."

David paced back and forth. "I've been leading the Warband to do our hunting since I became a warrior on my fifteenth year. That has been two years now. Because of the battles that I've won with the beasts, I truly believe that I could be of better use out there."

Patrick shook his head. "Not so. Your first responsibility is to the colony. If something should happen to me, the Dins won't be without a high prince and warlord."

Winifred sat down on a chair and stared at her husband. "I'm not eager to see you leave, but our population keeps dwindling."

Patrick paced back and forth. He stopped, faced Winifred, and threw up his arms. "That's why I have no other choice. I must do this. We've dwindled from millions to several hundred thousand."

Winifred sobbed into her hands. "Why have we waited so long? Why wasn't something done by our great-ancestrals? Now, you have to risk your life, because they did nothing."

"I knew you'd understand," Patrick said. He bent over, cupped her face with his hands, and gave her a kiss. "I'll be back as soon as I inform the others; it will take about a fortnight to make all the necessary arrangements. We must be well prepared."

For the next fortnight, the Elfdin colony prepared for the high prince's absence and planned for his journey. The Crusaders needed to travel light, but well-armed at the same time. Patrick had chosen his members of the crusade wisely. Warrior Archer was their keenest eyed warrior.Warrior Gwent was noted as the one who had killed more Krogs than any other warrior. Warrior Fletcher would be necessary to make arrows and bows, if needed. Warrior Dylan was almost as proficient with herbs and natural medicine as Master Drew and Mistress Meredith. Warrior Falconer had the best trained falcons that would be necessary to keep in touch with the colony. Besides having the best trained falcons known to the Dins, he was almost as keen-eyed as Archer with an arrow. If they were to be ready to defend themselves, they would need a couple of squires, warrior trainees, to carry the supplies. The best selections were Owen, Dylan's lad and Kevyn, Gwent's lad.

As the time drew close for the Crusaders to leave, the spirit of the Elfdin colony was higher than it had been in centuries. There had not been any jubilation since the Krogs' invasion. Already Warrior Bard, the minstrel, was singing their songs of triumph. A climate of triumph raised high, the first in many years. It was like King David and all the house of Israel dancing before the Lord when the Israelites brought the Ark of the Covenant into Jerusalem.

Although Patrick was pleased to see the elation, he felt too uncertain of the outcome to actually join in. He wanted to believe the ballads of Bard about victory, but he had no knowledge of the Great Forest beyond the Ravine surrounding Gold Mountain.

Foremost, he knew the wickedness of the Krogs. Dins were no match to the strength of the evil beasts if they encountered a multitude on their journey.

During the time of the Krogs, prayer to the Sovereign God had become story bound.Since they saw no bright white light, the people forgot about him. Lately, Patrick kept remembering something his ancestral-ma used to sing to him when he was a bairn; *"The Sovereign God shines his great light and causes evil to take its flight."* The words pierced his heart with a power that he had never sensed before. He decided to see if Great Prophet Drew knew what the words meant.

He found Drew at home and recited the words. "Do you have any idea what they mean? It is beyond me. My ancestral-ma died while on the hunt when I was quite young, and I had never asked her what the words meant."

Drew rubbed his chin with his right hand and mumbled the words over and over. "I have no idea what they mean." He hung his head. "If I had the correct lineage, I would most certainly know what it means." He grabbed his head with both hands. "I just feel so inadequate. My deficiency is hindering this colony."

Patrick folded his arms. "We could all say that we lack. Truth be told, there isn't anyone in this colony that can claim to have supernatural power flowing through them. But concentrating on our lack is not going to help any of us to conquer this thing if we allow ourselves to be overcome with our deficit. Besides, you can't be blamed for what your great-ancestrals did."

"I understand that. But I can make sure that my children have the right ancestry, and that's why I married your sister. Of course, we have loved each other since we were squires."

Patrick placed his right hand on Drew's left shoulder and looked him in the eyes. "Look, whether or not you have the right lineage, the Sovereign God still made sure that you have the physical requirements. You know that all great prophets and great prophetesses are three foot six inches tall with raven black hair and emerald green eyes. It is obvious that he chose you to be our great prophet." He gestured with both hands. "At present, we have to concentrate on getting our supernatural power back and defeating the Krogs once and for all."

"I know your right about the physical requirements." He bit his bottom lip. "I don't understand why He did that; however, I am truly grateful. But I do agree that the most important thing is getting our supernatural power back."

"Okay." Patrick said, rubbing his right temple. "Do you have any idea why we no longer pray to the Sovereign God?"

"All I can say is that we have no records in our possession. Everything vanished the day the Krogs appeared. After the beasts, all attention was given to physical warfare. It's like we just became so mindful of the use of physical weapons and defense tactics that we forgot how to use any supernatural power that we had. Now, we don't know how to. In fact, any Elfdin who knew anything about the Sovereign God is long dead. All we know is that his presence was a beautiful white light, bright, and warm." Drew cleared his throat and took a step forward. "My high prince, I'll be accompanying the Crusaders to the Gold Temple." He put his right hand up before Patrick could respond. "I know that won't rest easy with you, but I believe that I must."

Patrick's face screwed up in puzzlement. "Why do you believe that you must come?"

"I think it's a picture or something that I see in the back of my memory. I keep trying to bring it up, but it's buried too deep. I see bits and pieces that make no sense. I feel that I should know about it, but it's unclear. It was when I was a bairn, I think. Whether painted in my memory by the words of my ancestral-ma or whether just in my mind's eye, I really don't know. But I believe it has something to do with the Sovereign God and the Gold Temple. My mind sees giants and strange things that I don't recognize." He paused and gave a puzzled look. "Of course, Humans would seem like giants to us."

Patrick pondered what he heard. He didn't want to endanger the Dins' spiritual leader. But if Drew could help them, they needed all the help they could get. After all, he is a well-trained warrior. "I'm not in the place to tell our great prophet what to do; you're our spiritual leader. All I can say is that we're leaving at daytime. As long you can be ready by the time we leave, you're welcome to join us."

Drew gave a slow grin. "That won't be a problem. I packed three days ago and asked my family not to say a word to anyone. But I was waiting for the right time to speak to you alone. I felt the situation was serious enough for you to take me." He paused and bit his bottom lip. "All I know is that I have a really strong sense that I must join the Crusaders."

Patrick folded his arms with a chuckle. "I probably should've asked you to come. After all, in the old days, you would've been leading and not me." He turned to leave, but stopped short. "One more thing, you'll have to meet us in the Great Hall at night-time."

Patrick gathered the Crusaders together at nighttime for a last-minute briefing. "The Krogs will not expect us to be out at daytime. They know that we do our hunting at nighttime. If we can catch them off guard, we may be able to avoid detection." He reached into a pouch and handed out charcoal. "Make sure this covers your face, hands, and arms. We'll put a brown mesh cloak over our clothes to help camouflage our forest green outfits. Once we're outside the tunnel, we'll stay in the underbrush. I know they have scouts watching the tunnel, but no Din has gone out during the daytime for centuries. Let's hope they're slack during that time. We must move carefully, quietly, and as quickly as safety allows. If there are no questions, we'll relocate to the tunnel and head for the underbrush just before daytime."

Everyone was up and ready about an hour before daytime, gave their hugs and kisses, and headed for the tunnel which went from the top of the mountain down into the Ravine. Warriors were always on duty to guard the tunnel and keep the Great Flame burning. The first guard was ready to report. "My high prince, we've heard no Krog movement for some time now. Everything is quiet out there, just as we expected."

"Thanks. We'll need those on duty to be on the lookout while we slip out."

Warlord Patrick led the Crusaders to the end of the tunnel and turned to Great Prophet Drew. "Are you sure about this? We're all entering into unknown territory." He gestured with his hands. "We have no idea what is out there, or what we might encounter."

"I don't know what I am or what I am not. What I do know is that something deep inside is driving me on. I must go whether or not I am sure."

Patrick patted Drew's right arm. "Fair enough," he said before directing his attention toward the warriors on guard duty. "Okay, warrior guards, it's time for you to get the Great Flame moved aside so we can exit." Next, he addressed the Crusaders. "Okay, let's move out, move quickly, and move quietly. Follow behind me one by one. We'll head straight for the underbrush and stay close together. Once in the underbrush, we'll just crouch down till everyone is out." He motioned with his right hand. "Remember, not a sound."

They slipped mutely out of the tunnel and crawled into the underbrush. Patrick sensed the excitement and fear of the others. No Elfdin had ventured into the Great Forest in centuries. Questions rose in his heart like a rising river. What's out there? Does the ballad really give the directions to the temple? Do the Krogs inhabit it? Dins were in danger of extinction. Would the Humans still exist? Would there be any Humans who knew about the Elfdins and Oralee? Would the Portal still be there? Does the Gold Temple really exist?

His contemplation was interrupted as Archer touched his right shoulder and whispered in his right ear. "My high prince, I'm the last one out."

Patrick's heart raced as he looked at the group behind him. He stood, motioned with his right hand for them to get up, and placed his finger on his lips for silence. He picked up his pack and put his arms through the shoulder straps to secure it on his back. The others followed suit, and upon Patrick's leading, they started their journey to the Gold Temple.

In the Great Hall, the high prince's family, Winifred, Catrin, David, and High Druid's family, Meredith, Griffin, Meghan, and Vanora all sat with heads hung. Any message from the Crusaders would be delivered there. It was a solemn group. The spirit of jubilation had somehow dwindled. A fortnight there and a fortnight back would be a long month.

Catrin gestured with her right hand. "Ma, it's a month of traveling. Will they be at the Gold Temple long?"

"I can't answer that. I don't believe anyone knows, but let's hope not. After all, we have no idea what's out there. It's most addling." She gave a heavy sigh. "There's nothing we can do, except stay busy, or we'll all be wild with fright."

"Wait a minute!" Catrin exclaimed, looking around, "Where's Rhonda?"

David threw up his hands. "You know Rhonda; she's always checking something. Before the Crusaders left, she said she wanted to make sure the Great Flame was still burning after they went into the Ravine."

"That girl," said Winifred with a laugh, "she is truly a spiritual mentor in all aspects without the supernatural power."

All the others laughed.

"Excuse me," Griffin said. "Isn't it time for our spring repairs? Why don't we get all able-bodied warriors and squires to repair the colony? Such a task will help keep minds on something other than those on their way to the Gold Temple. Furthermore, all the noise should keep the Krogs' attention focused on us, so they don't get wise to the Crusaders."

David shook his head in agreement. "You're going to make a great spiritual leader. That's a fantastic idea." David rubbed the back of his neck. "Our high prince told me to make sure the Warband does their usual hunting. He said to have everyone go about business as usual. Anything abnormal on our part could alert the beasts and endanger the crusade. Our spring repairs are as normal as we can be."

Evil Druxin and Raven were busy making plans for Evil's takeover of Oralee and the Elfdins. "Once I'm great prophet, I'll use my skill in dark power to rule. First I'll destroy all the gold crosses representing the Sovereign God at the Gold Temple." He gave out a piercing laugh. "But my greatest pleasure will be demolishing the large Gold Cross covering the Portal entrance for the Humans. I must make sure none of them ever get back in; for most of them should still be alive. They are the only ones who know me and could hinder our revenge." He fingered his black beard. "I'll replace all crosses with the ones that I've made that say, *God Druxin*." He did a little dance and clapped his hands. "All of Oralee will think that I'm the Sovereign God." He smiled at Raven. "After you and the elders make sure the officiating great prophet, great prophetess, and their lad are destroyed, I'll no longer have any rivals." Twisting his right eyebrow, he grinned. "Of course, you must be sure to keep the lovely and spirited Catrin for me. After all, the great prophet is supposed to marry the high prince's daughter."

He walked over to a huge black chest and opened the lid. He carefully removed a protective cover and pulled out a white dress of satin and lace. It was embroidered with pearls along the hem, wrist, and neckline. "This was the dress that my Ma wore when she married my Pa. My wife will wear this," he said laying the dress on top of the chest as he sat in a nearby chair.

Raven rubbed his face on Evil's leg. "Yes, my friend, you shall share in my glory. I shall turn you into the second most handsome Din and train you in the ways of dark power. All of Oralee will gladly make you their high prince."

With a hissing sound, Raven's back raised high and stiff. Evil laughed. "Don't worry; you and the elders will make sure that the lower ranks eliminate the present high prince, high princess and their lad. The same rule holds true. As high prince, you shall have the fair Meghan to wed." An expression of satisfaction revealed itself in Evil's eyes. "I think I shall also give the privilege of transformation to the elders, Carbon, Nightshade, and Soot, your first litter in Oralee and the most like you and Little Coal. Oh yes, we will have to do away with the spiritual mentor and his lad; for

Carbon will do fine as the next spiritual mentor with the lively Rhonda by his side. I think Kevyn will make a suitable match for Nightshade. As for Soot, I haven't made up my mind which lad will be hers."

He rested his chin in his right hand with a solemn look. "I believe it may have been because Little Coal was carrying your first litter before entering Oralee that they are so like you two. But since that litter, the other litters you both had are nothing like either one of you." Evil jumped up and shook his fists, "She'd be alive if I had not been so eager that blasted Feast Day. I should have realized that you and she were not aware of the Dins ability to protect themselves in those days."He took the gown from the chest and sat down with it on his lap. "But I've paid my debt to her. I've kept you and those three close by my side and let the others do the fighting." He took a deep breath and stood up, while gently holding the gown. "You four will all rule under me and there will be no more fighting."

He stooped over the chest, gently placed the gown back in place, carefully covered it, and closed the chest. He straightened himself with pride. "This time I know I'm powerful enough to win." Evil patted Raven's head and stopped suddenly. "Now, that I think about it, it seems that all litters from everybody since that first litter have become more and more wild beast than pet.It's like all trace of Little Coal and you have disappeared in them." With a shrug of his shoulders, he laughed. "But they do the job quite well in eliminating the Elfdins. However, we'll have no need for them once we rule Oralee. We will have no more destruction of Dins."

Chapter 4

The Crusaders

PATRICK HOPED, ONCE OUTSIDE the Great Forest and in the Gold Valley, there would be underbrush to hide in. How far that would be, he didn't know. Travelling had become slow and tedious. He stopped to walk behind to make sure everyone was close. Drew was at his side as he walked by them all. In front were Squire Owen, then Dylan, then Squire Kevyn, then Falconer, then Fletcher, then Gwent, and finally Archer. All seemed to be in good temper. He leaned toward Drew. "Great prophet, we have to keep close and give no place for those beasts to separate us. Our best bet would be to find any cave-like crevasse to keep low and camp there. However, if there aren't any, I believe that it would be wise to stay under fallen trees and pile the brush up on top when we camp and watch the trees closely. I'm not sure if they hide in them."

Motioning them on, Patrick was taken aback by a hissing sound. Less than a foot behind him the evil beast had snuck up behind them. As he turned around, two sinister eyes stared at him. He no sooner saw it, when a vicious claw swung at him. He managed to jump out of the way, but his movement caused him to fall into Drew who fell into Archer. As the beast went to pounce on them, Gwent shot its left limb. With a screech, the beast turned to attack Gwent. Before he could grab another arrow, he jumped out of its way and fell backwards into Fletcher and Falconer. Kevyn was in its way and didn't move fast enough. It hit Kevyn with such force that he was knocked into Dylan who dropped his bow while falling against Owen. In the confusion, the beast leapt through the air toward the high prince who had just managed to stand up. Before the Krog had a chance to land on Patrick, an arrow came from behind them and hit the beast in the neck. The beast jerked in mid-flight and fell. Archer, now standing, was able to follow with an arrow between its eyes. Gwent, Fletcher, and Falconer managed to stand up and were getting their arrows ready when the beast fell. It would attack no more Dins. Archer helped the great prophet up. Outside of some scratches, all seemed fine.

Patrick motioned for all to stand in a circle, ready for another attack. After several minutes, with no other Krogs in sight, they lowered their weapons. Patrick stared at the beast in silence, and then he turned to the others. "If they find the carcass, they'll know we're on the move. Let's bury it deep and cover the carcass with the dirt. Then pile wet leaves and branches over the grave and pile limbs and branches on top for several yards around to camouflage the area."

Archer interrupted Patrick. "Excuse me, my high prince, but who shot the beast before me?" He pointed behind them. "The arrow came from that direction."

They all turned to look behind Archer, and Patrick yelled, "Whoever you are, show yourself or we'll all fire."

They all had bows ready, when Rhonda stood up.

Patrick was beside himself, and yelled. "What in Oralee are you doing here?"

Rhonda walked over to the Crusaders and placed her hands on her hips. "I wanted to be with Owen; I considered that if he required help, I'd be in attendance. However, it appears that my Pa was the one that necessitated help," she said, matter-of-factly.

Owen looked at her and then at the high prince. "I am innocent of any scheming; this has quite astonished me."

Drew bit his bottom lip and shook his head. "We can't take her back after traveling two days, and we certainly can't send her back alone."

Patrick folded his arms. "If this isn't dangerous enough, I have to be concerned about my thirteen-year-old lass."

Rhonda stuck out her chin. "Your thirteen-year-old lass is a trained squire just like thirteen-year-old Owen."

Tracing the scar from his right temple to his chin with his fingers, Patrick's voice was firm. "You had better stay close to Owen and Kevyn, and no more heroics. Do you understand?"

Rhonda looked down at the ground. "Yes, Pa." It took much self-control not to show her elation; for she was part of the Crusaders.

Journeying through the Great Forest on the third day, the Crusaders' travel was slowed almost to a halt. Patrick hadn't anticipated that the Great Forest would be so dense. Of course, no Din had traveled in the Great Forest for about four hundred years. Yet, he was overwhelmed at the tangle twisted mass of vines and how smothered the woodland seemed the farther west they went. Cutting through such overgrowth slowed them down. Maybe it was to their advantage. It meant no Krogs had traveled through this part of the Great Forest.

"I sure hope that we can get through this forest in time to make it to the Gold Temple in a fortnight," Fletcher said, wiping sweat from his forehead.

"I concur," Dylan remarked.

"Well," Drew said, taking a drink from his flask, "we just have to keep pressing forward."

Archer laughed. "That's definitely what we're doing."

Patrick was glad they encountered no Krogs the next couple of days of travel. Plodding through the underbrush had them exhausted. On the seventh day, they were entering a clearing at the end of the Great Forest, when the high prince was halted by Archer's exclamation. "Wow! Look at the size of that shadowy object. What is it?"

Drew stood with a dazed expression. "My high prince that is one of those things I keep seeing in my mind. I think it's a Human hut. Something like that is what I tried to explain. I believe that we are entering Gold Valley."

Suddenly, Patrick felt unequipped for what he witnessed. He knew Humans were like giants, but this was beyond his greatest imagination. Nevertheless, he was the warlord and high prince and must take control of the situation. He tried not to alarm the Crusaders and motioned for everyone to crouch down and form a circle. "We'd better be careful. The Krogs might inhabit it now."

Astonished and frightened by the huge edifice, he tried to regain his wits. Except for believing that it was a Human hut, Patrick had no idea that the peculiar sight he'd just viewed was a medieval castle. Although this particular one was not as large as what they would see, it was quite palatial with its many-sided tower. The mote and drawbridge were not built as a means of protection, but were merely the owner's preference. Any need for defense in the Golden Age, when Humans lived in Oralee, was unnecessary and unheard of.

High Prince Patrick stood slowly and viewed the countryside to consider their route through the valley. He didn't want them near the huge construction and what might occupy it.Nodding for them to stand, he pointed to his left. "I think we can still head west if we stay between those large stones and keep low. I believe that we have a few more hours of daytime." He folded his arms and laughed. "That is if you want to call this dreary atmosphere daytime; the ancestrals say that in the old days, daytime was a bright light." He rubbed his scar with his fingers. "Enough of what was, we better keep moving if we're going to arrive at the Gold Temple in a fortnight." He turned toward Drew. "Great Prophet Drew . . ."Before he could finish, there was a grinding sound, a loud crash as something struck the ground, then the thumps of Krogs on the run. With fear of the unknown, Patrick and the others hit the ground. "On your stomachs with heads raised, and make ready your bows," he whispered. His words were diminished as something ran from the Human hut.

Whatever creatures were heading toward them, Patrick was certain they weren't Krogs. He didn't recognize the strange, growling, low pitched sound, like a Din's stomach when hungry. "Growl," muddled the creature. It was not only unknown, but it was quite frightening. Lying on his stomach, every muscle tensed as he aimed an arrow in the direction of the sound. What was he to do? His heart beat faster, until his body was trembling. He tried to calm himself. Perhaps the new creatures wouldn't sense the Dins were there. "Growl, growl, growl," roared the creatures. The ground around him began to quake as they came closer. Patrick knew he must take control of his emotions and was about to blow the war horn, when he heard the loud shrieking wails of Krogs in battle. What were they fighting?

The ground was rumbling from the loud thumps as something pounded the earth. Every so often, one of the unknown creatures would yelp as if hurt. But Patrick knew the high-pitched screeches were Krogs in defeat. No victory sound came from the beasts; they were at war with a superior enemy..

Drew listened attentively as the battle wound down and knew that the Krogs were being defeated. He touched Patrick's right arm and whispered. "How will we ever fight things more frightening than Krogs? What should we do? Should we try to go back?"

Patrick rubbed the scar from his right temple to his chin. "We've come too far to turn back now. Besides, if we don't do something, we will become extinct. It's better to try and fail than to do nothing like our ancestrals did. I'm convinced that the days of doing naught are over."

Drew rubbed his chin with his right hand. "Of course, you are right. I felt that I was to come on this crusade, and I'm determined to stick it out to the end. If we don't try, we cannot overcome."

David was starting to worry about his Pa and the rest of the Crusaders. Things became more frightening when the warriors guarding the tunnel informed that another squire had slipped out the tunnel before they could replace the flame. They had no idea who it was with all the charcoal and the mesh cloak, until David went to see what was taking Rhonda so long to check on the Great Flame. High Princess Winifred was beside herself with fright, but the message the second nighttime from the Crusaders said that Rhonda was safely with them.

Outside of the message on the second nighttime about Rhonda, there has been no word for three days. Surely, they should know that the colony would be anxious about the crusade and the Crusaders. Why haven't they sent another message? David tried to calm himself by keeping everyone busy repairing the colony, but his heart grew heavier each day. Keeping his concern to himself, he addressed his Ma and sister as usual. "Ma, Catrin, I have to check with the Warband for tonight's hunting. I'll leave you both in charge. Tell the squires to meet me in a couple of hours for their assignments. Oh yes, if you see Griffin, tell him that I need to see him."

"Before you get too busy," Winifred said, "will you check the Great Hall for a message from your Pa? I know he said they wouldn't send the falcons too often for fear the Krogs would get suspicious. But I didn't think he meant it to be this long? Besides, Rhonda being with them has kept me from getting much sleep."

David gave a blithe motion with his right hand. "If I know Pa, he'll wait till they reach the Gold Temple. Believe me, if something had happened, the falcons would've returned."

"You're right," his Ma said with a sigh. "He'd be tactful. That's why he put you in charge while he's away. You, too, will make a rational and intelligent leader."

David walked away feeling anything but rational or intelligent. He was more affrighted than he liked to admit. His mind was racing with questions. What if the falcons had been destroyed with the Crusaders? How would he ever find out? His Pa's the high prince and warlord of the Elfdins, and he told him to rule in his stead. How could he rule the Dins? He was having enough trouble commanding his own emotions. He felt like a frightened squire seeing a Krog for the first time. What had his Pa meant about the Sovereign God dispelling evil? Was there anything that could dispel the evil of the beasts? He wished he knew. That's why he decided to talk to Griffin? After all, he was the future great prophet.

His thoughts were interrupted when Catrin came running up behind him. "David, I have to talk to you. I haven't spoken a word to Ma. She would only get more affrighted. Something keeps coming to my mind. Maybe I'm in a dither. But I can't shake it." Before he could speak, she continued. "And don't lecture me about being a silly female. You know that I believe in being sensible at all times. But we've only received one message from the Crusaders. That was their second night out. I don't like it."

"Pa said that it wouldn't be often. Falcons flying in and out of the tunnel would be too noticeable. The Krogs could follow it back to the Crusaders."

She place her hands on her hips. "I'm aware of all that, but that's not my problem."

"What is it then?" His voice became irritated. "I really don't have time. I have to meet with the Warband."

"I'll get to the point." She looked around to make sure they were alone. "What if the Krogs got them all, including the falcons? I know you calmed Ma down with your words of wisdom, but I'm not so easily fooled."

David, taken aback by his sister's remark, stood silently. He looked away and tried to think of something to say. His mind was blank. Since he couldn't think of an excuse, he decided to level with her. "I've been thinking the same thing. My mind has been in turmoil with no one to talk to. Right now, I have to choose warriors and squires from the Warband for tonight's hunt." He walked away, paused and looked over his shoulder. "Don't mention this to anyone, and we'll talk more after I get back from the hunt. In the meantime, you keep close to Ma. She needs encouraging support right now."

Evil had gathered Raven, Carbon, Nightshade, and Soot for last-minute instructions. He sat fingering his beard as he outlined their strategy on the map. "Each of you will lead an army of five thousand toward the Gold Temple. You all must be careful, for it's imperative that we encounter no hindrances." He picked up his oak shillelagh, waved it in a circular motion and spoke the words necessary to invoke an impenetrable shield around each. "Que Qui Omuk Omok Moka Muka." He grinned. "Now, you'll all be invincible to any attack. I'll not lose one of you like I did Little Coal."

He took an object from his pouch. It was a crystal shaped like a star. "I think I'd better check on the colony before we head out. I don't want any surprises at the last minute." Placing the crystal on a small tripod made of silver, he slowly moved his hands back and forth over it. First with the left hand going under the right hand and then the left hand going over the right hand as he chanted the spell. "Zar Zie Koqui Keeque Kayon." Raven, Carbon, Nightshade, and Soot all stood on hind legs with front paws resting on the table and watched the crystal.

Evil smiled as the colony came into focus. "It looks like spring cleaning is in full force." He looked at his audience and laughed. "The fools have no idea of what is about to befall them." He hesitated and blinked with confusion. "Something doesn't feel right. I'd better take a closer look." As the Warband appeared, they were busy making plans for the hunt. "Nothing strange there. What is it?" Meghan's face appeared as she helped her Ma with the cleaning. Raven hissed and stared at Evil. "Yes," he laughed. She's the one for you, and you shall have her." He spoke some more words and Catrin focused into view. "Remember that face. I'll not have a hair on her head harmed. She shall be mine." He twirled his right eyebrow and snarled. "Won't that be a slap in the face to the Sovereign God? I'll be great prophet and continue the line as it should have been four hundred years ago." He looked at Catrin. "My little pretty, you shall be the Ma of a new race of great prophets more powerful than even the Humans can fathom."

Chapter 5

The Sovereign God

CATRIN WAS WAITING FOR David in the Great Hall. She couldn't go to bed with a restless mind. Why was she so troubled? What was wrong with her? Were the Crusaders in danger? Was she allowing fright to rule her senses? She knew her Pa was the best warrior the Elfdins had; it had become hereditary since the Krogs. Perhaps, it was Rhonda being out there. The little rascal had more mettle than Catrin ever thought. She knew that her sister was much like her, but even she, herself, didn't think of such a venture. However, she could take solace in the fact that no Din has ever outshone the high prince in warfare since the Krogs. How could she allow herself to be so fainthearted? This is not like her; she needed to conquer her fears. With her mind so addled, she really needed to speak with David. She laid her head on her arms and fell asleep from sheer exhaustion.

Towing enough meat to feed the colony for some time, the warriors returned within a few hours. Jubilation, over the best hunt in sometime, had the Warband doing their dance of victory. Not only did the prey seem to be waiting, but there were no Krogs on duty. David hoped the beasts weren't tracking the Crusaders. His heart was in turmoil as they gathered in the Great Hall. But he managed to give everyone directions concerning the kill. The squires were to get it prepared as the warriors got the smokers going. At daytime, female warriors would put it into the stone cellar down in the mountain to keep it cool.

After he dispersed them, David spotted Catrin sleeping at the high prince's table. He walked to the front of the Hall and gently shook her right shoulder. "Catrin, what are you doing here at this hour? Did you plan to wait for me all night?"

She yawned and rubbed her eyes. "You're all back early. I didn't expect you back for hours."

"A freaky thing happened tonight. We encountered no Krogs and caught enough meat to last more than a month. But it was more eerie than it's ever been." He hesitated and gave a quizzical expression. "Does Ma know you're here?"

"No. She was in a deep sleep. Your words put her heart at ease, and she gave into her fatigue. I tried to rest, but concern for the Crusaders had me in its clutches. Rather than pace and wake her, I slipped out quietly." She yawned again. "I knew this is where you come after the hunt."

David sat beside her and gave a heavy sigh. "I've been in a dither for quite a while. I hoped that it was me, but I couldn't shake the feeling. Since the Krogs, no Din has traveled more than a few hours away from the tunnel to the left or to the right in the Ravine. I wasn't sure if the unknown had me worried. But it seems to be something that I can't put my finger on. It's some kind of strong feeling that I don't understand. Tonight's happenings make matters worse. Everything was too unusual for me. The Warband thought it was great, but I don't like it." He rubbed the back of his neck with his right hand. "I have this strange feeling deep inside and I don't know what to do."

Catrin jumped up suddenly. "Never mind all that. I have something to tell you. While waiting for you, I fell asleep." She looked around and lowered her voice. "Something I've never seen shone on me and I heard words. It was a beautiful white light, bright, and warm. My whole being can still feel the warmth of the words. 'You and David are my warriors, and I want you to travel to the Gold Temple. You must not tarry a moment.'" She placed her right hand on his left shoulder. "I believe it was the Sovereign God."

David's eyes bulged. "He spoke to you? No Din has heard from him in centuries."

"I've made up my mind. I'm going to find Pa and Rhonda. Don't try to stop me. I may be a female, but I'm trained as a warrior. Ever since the Krogs, the females have been trained as diligently as the males. I know many of us have never actually battled since Arwyn's death, but we are disciplined. That's all any of the Warband were before they went out the tunnel." She twirled her hair with her right forefinger. "Besides, the Sovereign God wants us to go."

"I know Pa told me to stay," he said, walking back and forth. "But he never told me to stay, if an emergency said to leave." He stopped and folded his arms. "That's it. I'm not dickering with this any longer. Let's get packed and leave."

"I've already packed for the two of us," Catrin laughed. "But we'd better tell Ma."

Neither David nor Catrin perceived three silhouettes behind the veil where the great prophet sat. They had slipped in while Catrin was sleeping and Griffin felt not to wake her.

Griffin had not intended to eavesdrop. But he felt that once David and Catrin started their conversation, it was better if they didn't know that it wasn't private. He motioned for his sisters to sit quietly until they left. Along with Meghan and Vanora, he listened attentively. He and Meghan were packed; it had been their intention to make similar plans. They, too, were troubled about the Crusaders. Griffin couldn't wait for the two to leave. His emotions were racing. How could they join the quest? He was intrigued about Catrin's dream. "Wait till Pa hears that the Sovereign God spoke to Catrin. This is mind boggling." He tapped his lips with his right forefinger. "Okay, this is what we'll do. Once they are away from the tunnel, we'll follow behind before the guards move the Great Flame back into place."

He gazed at his sisters and felt sad for Vanora. "We hate to leave you, but you'd never make such a journey. If you lost the bairn, Archer and Pa would never forgive us. Besides, Ma already told you that she intends to stay with you."

Vanora looked at him with her mouth turned down at the corners and spoke softly. "I know folly won't help Archer, Pa, or the others. I'll do the right thing and stay in the colony. This bairn means too much to us; I won't risk anything happening to it." She gave a chuckle. "Besides, I can't seem to get around my belly to do much of anything these days."

Griffin stood up and clasped his hands. "Okay, we have all our gear with us. Let's hide behind the tall object nearest the tunnel and watch for David and Catrin to go in. We'll wait and follow them out and lay flat in the underbrush until they leave. They have no idea that we know, so they won't be checking to see if anyone is following."

Meghan twisted her hands. "I can't believe that I'm doing this. But this feeling inside is too strong to ignore. I can't explain it, but I know that I must do this." She took a deep breath. "Okay, let's go."

Catrin told her Ma about her dream and what they had to do. Winifred listened with tearful eyes. With a heavy sigh, she hugged them. "I really want to stop you both, but something inside me is telling me to let you go. Maybe it is the Sovereign God stopping me. All I know is that I must let you go." She grabbed her head with both hands. "I just wish Rhonda hadn't been so fool-hearty. However, I know you two must do what you believe the Sovereign God told you to do. I don't understand any of this, but it's like I'm not supposed to. I believe that what the Sovereign God says to do must be done."

Without a word, they ran to get their packs, bows and arrows, hunting blades, food, water and doubled checked to make sure that they had all they needed. Then they put the brown mesh cloak over their clothes, rubbed themselves with charcoal, and headed for the tunnel. David knew they'd startle those on guard duty, but he also knew they wouldn't question the future high prince. "We're heading to the Gold Temple," he said. "Our Ma is in charge while I'm gone. She'll explain what's what. There'll be no need to hunt for several weeks, but all other duties are to be carried out. Be sure to keep the Great Flame burning. That flame seems to be the only thing Krogs fear."

It was quiet as they crept out of the tunnel; there was not a Krog in sight. David thought it strange, but he was glad for their sakes. He didn't know what to think of his sister being with him. What will their Pa do when he sees them? Will they find the Crusaders alive? Why were they going? What was the Sovereign God doing? How come He was speaking after so many years? Was it really the Sovereign God, or a trick of the Krogs? After all, they had taken the Dins' supernatural power. Were they using it as an ultimate weapon to destroy them? Nothing made sense to him, except that he felt driven by a sense of urgency. It had nothing to do with Catrin's dream; it was that strong impression inside. Of course, her dream was the catapult to get him to finally move on what he was sensing.

David and Catrin made triple time. With a clear path made by the Crusaders, they reached the end of the Great Forest late the second evening and stopped short as they witnessed a strange shadowy object. Catrin climbed a tree to get a better view of the strange edifice in the clearing beyond. Like the Crusaders before her, she had never seen a castle. "I've no idea what it is. I wish it was lighter, so I could see more clearly. It's hard enough to see during daytime hours with the shroud, never mind nighttime. You don't suppose Pa and the others are trapped inside? How will we ever rescue them from such a place?"

David rubbed the back of his neck with his right hand. "We first have to ask if they're in there before we ask how. Let's both climb as high as we can. Then I'll blow the war horn. If Pa answers with his horn, then we can ask how." They both climbed high and sat on two separate branches. David was about to blow the horn, when he heard Krogs. They sat still to listen. An army of the beasts headed their way. Hoping it was too dark to spot them, they both froze in place. If they were seen, there was no way out. Fighting a few beasts is one thing, but an army is another.

Instead of continuing, the army stopped in the underbrush beneath the tree. David looked down and pointed at the Krogs. Catrin knew what he meant, she was sure that it was an army of thousands. They both sat stone still and watched what seemed as if the beasts were busy making plans and motioning toward the castle. All of a sudden, one of them stood quietly and began to sniff around. A few others did the same, until one looked up in the tree and gave a dreadful hissing noise. David's face told Catrin that he too sensed they were doomed.

Patrick composed himself and lifted his head to look at the rest. All had dropped down and lay face down hugging the ground for dear life. He thought he should get up to see what the beasts were fighting, but a cracking of branches nearby sent him face down. Next moment, he heard several run like the wind past them without a pause. Whatever they were that ran by, kept heading away, until Patrick heard the same grinding as before. However, on this occurrence, there weren't any loud slams or Krogs on the run.

There was silence for some time, when Patrick finally looked up. In the distance, he could make out the carcasses of Krogs deposited about the ground, but nothing moved. With snail-like motion, he stood up and perused the terrain. "Okay, Crusaders, we have to move on. Everything's been silent for quite a while; I don't see anything stirring. We'll do as I said earlier, keep to the large stones. I don't know what's out there, but I know the Krogs aren't too eager to tackle it. With the multitude of dead beasts out there, let's hope we don't have an encounter with the new creatures. There's not too much daytime left, but we've lost time. I think we better move as quickly as possible before nighttime takes over."

It was almost nighttime when the Crusaders came upon a cleft in a large stone with a cavity that went underground. Patrick checked things out. "This will make a good place to camp until daytime. We all need some sleep. After we eat, Archer, Rhonda, and I will take first watch. Dylan and Fletcher have the second, Gwent and Owen have third, and Falconer and Kevyn the last."

All was quiet, until Gwent and Owen's watch. Krogs had snuck up behind and attacked before they knew what happened. Patrick heard the commotion and was up in an instant with Fletcher, Falconer, and Archer right behind. They found Gwent in the clutches of one of the beasts and Owen cornered by two others. Before the Crusaders could shoot any arrows at the beasts, four more leapt from behind the stone. In a flash, Archer shot two arrows at the two beasts cornering Owen. One was fatally wounded, but the other turned its attention toward Archer. But he was too fast for it, and down it went with an arrow in its heart.

Archer turned his attention toward the beast with Gwent in its clutches. He hit another bull's-eye and down went the Krog, while Patrick, Drew, Falconer, Fletcher, Dylan, Rhonda, Owen, and Kevyn managed to get the four new beasts.

Archer had pulled Gwent out from underneath the beast, when ten more of the ugly fiends leapt from behind the rock. Patrick noticed more following behind them and gave orders to retreat. "Get back into the crevasse, we'll shoot from there and get a flame started." Archer had Gwent over his shoulder and was first back into the cavity. The others, shooting arrows, followed close behind.

In another tree, a few yards away from David and Catrin, sat Griffin and Meghan who had been following close behind. Watching the Krog army move in had them in turmoil. How would they rescue their high prince's heirs? Any attempt to fight an army would be their end. "I wish I knew the old prayers," Griffin whispered. "Our ancestrals would have known how to be delivered from things like this." He paused, scratching his head. "However, they had no need to be delivered from Krogs; they didn't exist back then. They lived in peace and prosperity; we only know how to be affrighted." He tapped his lips with his right forefinger. "David mentioned something to me about a song his great-ancestral-ma sang to his Pa about the Sovereign God dispelling evil."

"Yes, I heard high prince mention it to Pa when I brought them a pitcher of mead. But they waited for me to leave before continuing the conversation."

Griffin shrugged his shoulders. "Maybe I'm more affrighted than I know, but I'm going to try something. Anything has to be better than nothing at this time. We can't just sit and watch the Krogs destroy Catrin and David."

Meghan twisted her hands. "You're not going to do something fool hearty that could get the Krogs to notice us?"

Chapter 6

The Unknown Creatures

IT WAS NEARLY DARK when the Crusaders stopped to camp. Patrick hoped they'd see no Krogs. The last battle found them exhausted and barely escaping with their lives. Somehow, at daytime, the beasts were no longer there. Gwent had been badly wounded, and probably wouldn't have made it if Drew hadn't been there. Although Dylan had a way with herbs; he was no match to Drew's ability. As the great prophet, Drew was both spiritual leader and physical healer. He and Meredith both had a way with herbs and natural remedies that was almost supernatural.

Patrick was observing the area when he saw a huge shadowy structure. "Stop," he said. "What's that in front of us?" He rubbed the scar from his right temple to his chin. "I think it's another one of those Human huts that we found at the end of the Great Forest, but it's probably three times the size. Perhaps we better hide quickly, before we get into a jam too big for us to handle." He surveyed the situation quickly and pointed to his right. "Over there, it looks like fallen trees; they should hide us while we rest."

No sooner were they in hiding, when running creatures were headed their way. The stomps were too heavy for Krogs. Patrick tried to see what it was, but it was too dark. Giant shadows ran past without stopping, until they were almost out of hearing. The silence was short in duration. In no time, came the loud shrilling squeals of Krogs in battle. Like before, the beasts were losing. What were they fighting?

Patrick desperately wanted to run and see, but he was afraid of endangering the rest. He could hear the same growling sounds and something pounding the ground, along with the usual shrieks of the beasts. He was pleased to hear the Krogs being defeated. However, the thought of facing an enemy larger than the beasts made him more affrighted than he'd like to admit.

Again, the battle was short in duration. Within minutes, the same giant shadows ran past to Patrick's relief. "I think," Patrick said, "we better rest for a while. I don't know what's between us and the Gold Temple, but I'm not sure that I want to know. Because the beasts have always been fearless monsters, their fright worries me." He took a drink from his flask. "We'll start out again in about an hour and keep far away from that Human hut. I don't want to excite what might be in there."

To recover time lost struggling through the Great Forest and combating Krogs, the Crusaders decided to forego camping unless the respite was needed. Travelling daytime and nighttime, for several days, managed to get them back on schedule. Drew tapped Patrick on his right shoulder. "My high prince today is day thirteen of this Crusade. If the ballad is correct, we should see the Gold Temple tomorrow. Although we had a few setbacks, I believe we're on the proper timetable."

"I know. Excitement is swelling up inside me combating the fear. Let's hope the ballad is what we think. It seems too real, not to . . ." He stopped abruptly. "Wait a minute! Did I see something move to my right?"

"What?" Drew asked. "Move where?"

Before Patrick could answer, the ground beneath their feet moved. They were snared so swiftly that no one knew what happened. The Crusaders found themselves about twenty feet in the air, and trapped in a tightly woven net made of an unknown metal substance. Hunting blades wouldn't cut them loose from this prison. "Listen to me," Patrick said. "Is anyone hurt?"

"No," they all replied in unison.

"That's a relief. But if we don't move, someone might get hurt. I think we can all sit side by side. Whatever this thing is, it seems big enough. There's no sense staying piled on top of each other."

He waited for everyone to get settled before he tried to appraise the situation. "Falconer, I can't see anything in this dark. We have to figure a way to get down or get a falcon out. But then, again, we don't want anyone from the colony trying to come and rescue us."

Drew shook his head. "That's for sure, especially since we have no idea what the latest creatures are."

The Krogs were busy communicating with each at the base of the tree. It was obvious that Din supper was on the menu. David and Catrin had no way out. They watched in nervousness as the army gathered around the tree. Several had their eyes centered on the two warriors.

Catrin gestured down at the Krogs below. "David, it seems like more and more are coming. Look at those sinister eyes looking up at us. It's as if they can already savor their supper. They are such wicked beasts." She gestured with her right hand. "Maybe we should climb up higher to smaller branches. After all the beasts are much heavier, and they won't be able to stand on them without falling. Perhaps, they will quit after a while."

David rubbed the back of his neck. "I don't understand any of this. Maybe we should have stayed at the colony like Pa said."

"No!" Catrin clenched her right fist. "We were told to come. I can still feel the words that the Sovereign God said to me." She gestured with her right hand. "Let's climb up higher like I said."

They both climbed up as high as they could and balanced on small branches. When they looked down, they heard a Krog make a sound to the others as it was getting ready to climb the tree. Bows were set. The beasts weren't getting them without a fight. "Aim between the eyes," David said, "that's a sure winner. We'll get several before they get us."

Catrin shook her head. "Something is not right. We were told to go. I don't believe that this is our end. After all, the Sovereign God told us to go to the Gold Temple; we aren't there yet. Surely, he wouldn't have told us to go someplace if we weren't going to get there. I still believe that we will get to the Gold Temple; I can still feel his warmth whenever I mention him."

David stared in contemplation and gave out a loud sigh. "Well, we definitely need his help now."

Griffin could tell by the movement at the tree that the beasts were ready to climb it and attack David and Catrin. He didn't care if he sounded foolish to his sister. After all, if he could do something to help them, he was willing to do it. He would go to any lengths to save them. If anything happened to Catrin, he didn't know what he'd do.

In desperation, he cried out as loud as he could. "Sovereign God! Please hear me. I'm Griffin, the future great prophet of the Elfdins. I don't know you, but my high prince said that you are supposed to dispel evil. Krogs are as evil as they come. Meghan and I are powerless to help Catrin and David. I ask you to deliver the heirs of my high prince from the horrible beasts." When he finished, he leaned back against the tree. "Please protect Catrin," he whispered.

Meghan sat stone still on a limb and stared wide-eyed at him. She was too numb to speak.

Griffin saw her face and was grateful for her silence.

David screwed up his face in confusion. He knew Catrin had heard Griffin's plea by her baffled stare. But where had it come from? Surely it wasn't a trick of the Krogs; they wouldn't call on the Sovereign God to dispel them. What in Oralee was going on? Before he could decipher the situation, there was a loud grinding sound and a raucous crash as something hit the ground.

Catrin jumped at the sound and grabbed the branch above her. "Did you hear that? What is that sound? I've never heard the likes before."

David looked down. "I don't know what it is, but the Krogs seem to recognize it. Look at them, they're frantic and it seems that they've forgotten about their Din supper."

It was too dark to see anything clearly, but David and Catrin heard low growls and saw giant shadows nearing the trees. In a moment, were heard the shrieking wails of the beasts in battle.

David leaned toward Catrin's head and whispered in her ear. "Don't move the branches; we need to stand perfectly still. We don't want what's attacking the Krogs to know we're here. If I thought the beasts were huge, those creatures make them look small." He rubbed the back of his neck with his right hand. "If I thought an army of Krogs was too much to handle. I don't even want to think about a confrontation with these new creatures."

Catrin touched his right arm and whispered. "I know what you mean. What in Oralee is more powerful than Krogs?"

Griffin thought he was dreaming. He saw giant shadows attacking the Krogs. The beasts were in heavy battle. Their blood curdling squeals were nothing like he had ever heard. They were fighting a superior enemy. Krogs were screeching, scratching, and hissing to get away. As he watched in the darkness, Meghan touched his right arm. "Is that the Sovereign God? It came when you asked for help. Whatever it is, it's more powerful than anything we've ever seen."

Griffin scratched the back of his head. "I don't know what it is. All I know is that I'm grateful."

Just as quickly as the combat started, it was over. The beasts ran for the thickness of the Great Forest, and the growling giants headed away from it toward the Human hut. There was the same grinding noise as the beginning, and then all was quiet.

Griffin helped Meghan down from the tree. "Let's check on David and Catrin, I believe it's safe. The beasts are long gone.

Maybe we better join forces. We don't know what's out there." He exhaled. "I hope the Crusaders are safe."

As they reached the tree, they heard David and Catrin coming down. Griffin looked around before he spoke. "David, don't shoot. It's me, Griffin, and Meghan is with me."

"Well, that's a relief. I thought I was losing my mind." David got his bearing and stared quizzically at them. "What in Oralee are you doing here? How did you know where we were? It was you, who called on the Sovereign God, wasn't it?"

"We've been following you both."

Catrin threw her hands up. "But how did you know that we were leaving? I'm sure our Ma didn't tell you."

Griffin scratched the back of his head with his right hand. "I must admit that you weren't alone when you were talking in the Great Hall. Meghan, Vanora, and I had slipped in while you were sleeping, and I felt to let you sleep. When David came in, we were sitting at the great prophet's table behind the veil. We were having the same problem about the Crusaders. Meghan and I were packed and ready to go find the Crusaders. We were making last-minute plans, when David came in and started to talk to you. Once we heard what you were saying, I decided that it was best if we all remained quiet. We listened and figured that we would just follow you both out the tunnel and stay close behind. I figured if we told you, you wouldn't let us come." He clasped his hands and motioned towards David. "And yes, it was me. We were up in a tree several yards from here. When I saw the dilemma, I didn't know what to do. I remembered what you had told me about the Sovereign God and asked for his help."

Catrin put her right hand on his left shoulder and shook her head. "I don't know what happened, but I'm thankful that you asked. I was beginning to get a little affrighted." She gestured with both hands. "When the Sovereign God told me that David and I were to go to the Gold Temple, I didn't give any thought to the trouble we might face."

Griffin gazed eagerly at Catrin. He wanted to know more about what he heard in the Great Hall. "You know for sure that it was the Sovereign God who told you and David to go to the Gold Temple?"

"Yes. I was waiting for David. When I fell asleep, He spoke to me."

"How do you know it was the Sovereign God? Did you see him?"

"Yes and no, it was a presence. All I know is that it was a beautiful white light, bright, and warm; the warmth went all through me. As a matter of fact, I can feel him now. When I talk about it, I get that same warm sensation."

Griffin just shook his head in wonder. "I'm really boggled. This has to be the greatest thing I've heard in all my days." He clasped his hands. "I am all astonishment! Wait till great prophet hears this."

Catrin laughed and squeezed his right arm. "Aren't you a fine one for talking? You just got through calling on him. Wait till your Pa hears what you did. It was you calling on the Sovereign God that saved us from the Krogs."

"Okay," David interjected. "You two can laud one another later. Right now, I think we have to get out of the open. I saw a large fallen tree, when I first climbed up to view the Human hut. Let's get deep inside and build a barricade around ourselves with the branches. That should keep us safe for the night."

Catrin suddenly realized that Meghan was there. "Meghan what in Oralee are you doing here? Did you forget that there are Krogs out here?"

Meghan twisted her hands. "I know what you are thinking, but I just felt this impression that I had to go. I can't explain it."

"Wow!" David exclaimed. "That's what happened to me." He rubbed the back of his neck. "There are some strange happenings going on." He looked around and pointed his right forefinger to his right. "I believe that we had better get under that tree and pile branches and brush inside and out for protection."

Once they were settled in, they all ate and made themselves comfortable for the night. Griffin scratched the back of his head with his right hand. "We better get some sleep. This has been a tiring ordeal. We'll need our wits about us come daytime. We can't give place to fatigue and not be prepared for what's out there."

Meghan twisted her hands. "Particularly since we have no idea what those giant creatures are that can defeat Krogs. I mean really, where did they come from?"

Catrin just shook her head and sighed. "I sure hope we don't have to fight them. They're huge compared to the Krogs."

David made a bed with some leaves and placed his blanket on top. "Okay, let's all be quiet and get some rest."

Patrick tried to keep the Crusaders from being overwhelmed. Thoughts ran through his mind as he surveyed the situation. We have food and water for a few days. What am I doing? I can't let myself think like that. There must be a way to get out of this mess. But this net is a puzzle. I've never seen anything like it. "Is anyone familiar with a net like this?" He asked. "I've no idea what it is."

They all responded in unison. "No!"

"Anyway," Patrick said, rubbing the scar from his right temple to his chin with his fingers, "even if one of us did know about it, it's too dark to do anything. We better all get some rest. If we're not refreshed, we won't be able to think straight. I don't believe that we have to concern ourselves with a watch tonight. Krogs couldn't reach us, even if they tried. I guess that's a consolation." He was interrupted by heavy clomps heading their way.

"Oh no!" Drew said. "It's the other creatures, the growling ones. I hope they don't know we're here."

"Shush!" Patrick whispered. "Don't anyone make a sound. I don't believe they could reach us either, but I want to play it safe." In minutes, the thumps ran underneath them in the direction the Crusaders were supposed to be headed. Not a one stopped or slowed its pace.   "Whew!" Dylan said. "That was quite a scare. This expedition becomes extra scary each daytime."

Gwent nodded. "That's for sure."

Archer turned toward Patrick. "My Prince, how will we ever fight anything more powerful than Krogs?"

Fletcher leaned back against the net. "What I'd like to know is where they came from.How come we never saw them before?"

Patrick rubbed the scar from his right temple to his chin. "All I know is that it's obvious that Krogs know about them and are not too eager to confront them. I must admit that it's those new creatures that have saved us a few times from the Krogs. I don't understand why they haven't discovered us yet, but I guess I really don't care. All that I'm concerned with is that we make it safely to the Gold Temple."

"My high prince," said Archer, "they must be headed for the Gold Temple. But I can't understand why they don't sniff us out like the Krogs?"

Squire Rhonda beamed with revelation. "Perhaps they don't consume Dins!"

At that Owen chimed in. "I definitely concur."

Everyone just let out a laugh until their stomachs were shaking with laughter.

Patrick was relieved to hear them at ease, but he knew they were still in a dilemma."Okay, Crusaders, we really have to get some rest. Let's settle down for a while. We're going to need our wits about us come daytime. We've been traveling almost daytime and nighttime for several days to make up for lost time, and we could all use the rest."

David woke the others to Krogs trying to break down the wall of branches protecting them."Wake up! Krogs are trying to get in. Get your bows ready."

"What are we going to do?" Catrin asked. "They're all around us; we've no way out."

Fright revealed itself in Meghan's face. "We're no match against that many. What was I thinking to join this quest? I must be out of my mind." She let a heavy sigh. "This is too much of a jam for us to get out of."

Griffin motioned with both his hands. "Let's all stay calm. If we panic, we'll make the wrong move."

As he listened to the others, David's mind raced. Maybe they should've stayed in the trees, but that wasn't going to help them now. He'd better take control of the situation. "If they break through, we'll just have to fight to the end. They won't get us without a challenge."

Catrin clenched her teeth. "I don't believe that the Sovereign God would tell us to go someplace, unless we were going to make it. Whatever is going on cannot be our end. We must fight on and accomplish what the Sovereign God told us to do."

"Ouch!" Meghan yelled. "One of those beasts just clawed my arm; I can't believe that I'm here."

Catrin immediately aimed her bow. "Take that, you beast," she bellowed ferociously. Straightening herself with dignity, she turned to Meghan with a grin. "He won't scratch anyone again, not with an arrow between its eyes."

"Griffin! Watch out!" David shouted, as he shot over Griffin. "That beast almost grappled your head. I think we'd better get close together and form a circle. Let's stand shoulder to shoulder, so that we have someone looking in every direction."

Before they could take position, Catrin aimed over David's shoulder. David turned and smiled. "Good shot, Catrin. You finished that one, too." They no sooner formed the circle when David saw two Krogs about to break through. "Catrin, you take the left and I'll take the right." More beasts were reaching through with their villainous claws. David knew they weren't going to hold the beasts back much longer. "Maybe we better call on the Sovereign God again. He helped us last time. If he doesn't, we won't have to be concerned about the Crusaders. We'll all be dead."

Griffin nodded his head. "I've been thinking the same thing. Do you want me to do it?"

"Yes. It is you that is going to be the future great prophet. I believe it's always been our spiritual leaders that guide the way."

"Wait a minute." Meghan whispered. "I hear something running in our direction."

Everyone remained quiet to listen. Nearby were loud growling sounds. David knew it was the same giant creatures that fought the Krogs the night before. It was horrendous with the high pitch screeching of the Krogs, the pounding on the ground, and the growls of the unknown beings. David went to speak, but was interrupted as part of the barricade almost fell in from the weight of the pounding. "Everyone put your backs against the branches. Maybe we can keep them from caving in on us." He looked around to make sure everyone was in place. His eyes bulged at his sister. "Catrin! Brace yourself. Your side just moved."

Chapter 7

The Pundles

Morning found the Crusaders still twenty feet in the air and caged with no way of cutting through. Patrick, as always, was viewing the situation. Everyone was eating, so it gave him time to meditate. He remembered the ballad about the Sovereign God. *How do I even know if there is still such a being? If the Humans are extinct, maybe he's destroyed. Something has to be done, or we'll all starve to death in this net. I wish we had some knowledge about a God who dispels evil. We need his help.* He turned to inquire of Drew. "I wish we knew about the Sovereign God. Didn't the great prophet call on him?"

"I think so, but I don't know how. It's so shameful that we've forgotten so many of the old ways. Our people have slipped into ignorance concerning a lot of things. All our attention has been on physical warfare and survival since the Krogs that we're ignorant of supernatural power. I think that we need to find our Sacred Books to find out how to get our supernatural powers back."

Patrick gestured with his hands. "Well, we have to do something."

"I feel something inside saying the same thing. Okay, I'm going to do it. Just give me a minute to get my bearing. This is all new to me." He took a few deep breaths and sat up straight. "Here goes," he said, blowing out air. "Please hear me Sovereign God, I'm Drew, great prophet of the Elfdins. We really don't know you, but you're supposed to dispel evil. This net is evil. If we don't get out, we'll die. Please help us out of this, and please help us get to the Gold Temple so that we can find the Sacred Books that teach us how to worship you and how to get our supernatural power back."

There was no sound. It was so quiet that they could hear their own breathing. Patrick kept his eyes and thoughts toward the sky. Maybe the Sovereign God lives in the sky where the white light used to be. As he studied the area above his head, he noticed the net was secured by a thick twine rope, but the ends left an opening of about a foot in diameter. It was an incredible bit of ingenuity; it must have been what the Humans used for hunting. "Look everyone." He pointed up with his right forefinger. "Do you see the rope above us that's securing the net?"

Drew eyebrows scrunched together. "Yes. But what can we do? We can't reach it with our blades."

"Yes, we can. Listen to me, I have an idea. Let's everyone stand up slowly. I believe we can tie our ropes around the limb holding this net. Kevyn is the lightest; I'll have him stand on my shoulders to get our ropes over the limb. Once he has all the ropes secured, he'll have to cut the rope that holds the net. But first, we'll all have to twist our rope around a leg and hold on with both hands. Kevyn will twist the rope around his leg while standing on my shoulders and hold onto the rope with one hand. Once he's set, he'll cut the rope securing the net, and quickly grab his rope with the other hand. We must hold our rope tight, and I mean tight. When that rope snaps, all our weight will want to drop. We have to let the net drop around us and then let ourselves down easy."

Kevyn managed to get everyone's rope over the limb and secured. Then one by one they all held their rope with one hand and waited for Patrick to give the next instruction. Patrick had them twist their right leg around the rope and grab tight with both hands. "Okay, Kevyn cut the rope, let your blade fall outside and grab the rope tight. Make sure you retrieve your blade when we get down."

Kevyn took a deep breath. "Here goes. It's quite thick, but my blade is cutting through."

"There it goes," Falconer said.

All had their ropes gripped tightly as the net fell down around them; it landed on the ground with a thud. Patrick looked down to make sure no Krogs were around. "Okay, let's ease down. Remember, we must take it slow, one hand at a time." He paused as they all moved slowly down. "Great! We only have a few more feet to the ground. Easy does it, as we land. We don't want to trip on the net."

"We have accomplished it!" Owen and Rhonda exclaimed.

Patrick and Drew were the first to step away from the net. The others all followed, and Kevyn quickly retrieved his blade. Once everyone was clear, Patrick motioned for them to get out of sight before he spoke. "We've lost some time, again. That means that we're going to have to travel faster today to make up the lost hours. Is everyone ready to travel?"

Drew laughed. "I believe that we're all just as anxious as you to see the Gold Temple."

"That's for sure," Gwent laughed. "Don't believe any of us want to dawdle."

"Exceptional!" Rhonda exclaimed. "I consider that I'm accurate in deducing that we all contemplated a dreadful end."

The others all gave a chuckle of relief.

The battle was raging outside the stockade of branches and brush. The heirs of the high prince and of the great prophet were braced against the sides of the shelter. There was no question who was winning. Krogs were no match against the giant creatures that growled all around.

"Griffin!" David yelled over the noise. "We better get ready to combat the other creatures. Why don't we bury ourselves under the brush? When the sides cave in, maybe they won't be able to get us. What do you think?"

Stress lines formed on Griffin's brow. "We better do something. To me, it sounds like it might be winding down. The squeals of the beasts are getting fewer and fewer. I believe it's about over."

David waited for the sides to cave in on them as they all lay under the brush, but nothing happened. When he heard no sound for quite a while, he got up from the brush and listened carefully before speaking. "I think we're alone. This becomes more addling with every battle. I'll take a look around. Stay here, until I come back." He climbed out of the branches, walked around to the other side, and was startled by the biggest white creature he'd ever seen. Its head was cocked sideways, and two blue eyes just stared. Fearful for the others, he yelled. "Don't come out here. There's one of those giant creatures out here. Maybe I can crawl back in. Ouch! I can't breathe. Stop that. What are you doing? Ugh, you're getting me all wet."

Fear rose on the countenances of the three inside the barricade. All stood silently with eyes bulged. Catrin was the first to speak. "Why can't we hear David yelling from pain? What in Oralee is going on out there? I don't believe he's fighting the creature. What is he doing?"

Griffin motioned for the girls to stay calm. "Both of you stay here. I'll see what's going on."

Catrin followed behind him. "You're not the only one who has to see what's going on out there." She gestured with her right hand. "That's my brother out there. I'm following you out."

Meghan twisted her hands. "Me too. I mean, after all, David is the next high prince and I am the next high princess."

All three crawled out, walked around the tree and gazed in disbelief. Never had they seen such a giant white creature, nor could they believe what it was doing. It was washing David's face with the biggest tongue they'd ever seen. Catrin didn't know whether to cry or laugh, so she decided on the latter. "David, I think it likes you." She no sooner said that, when several more came running over. Like the first one, they knocked the Dins down and proceeded to wash their faces.

These Elfdins had never seen a Pundle, nicknamed Pun. All were boggled at the blue-eyed creatures. They didn't know they were viewing creatures that resembled a giant German-Shepherd with white hair. David finally managed to get up. He rubbed the top of his head at the sight of the others on the ground getting a face washing from the white creatures. "Why are these creatures so friendly to Dins but utterly destroy Krogs?" He gave out a laugh. "Hey, Griffin, Meghan, Catrin, just stand up. Don't worry, the creatures won't stop you."

After they all stood, the Puns started to run ahead to the left, and then run back. It was Catrin who realized what was going on. "They want us to follow them. We'd be crazy not to. They'll protect us from Krogs. As a matter of fact, I believe that's what they've done each time we've been attacked."

David knew there was no use making any plans of his own. "I don't know what's going on, but I'm following them." He rubbed the back of his neck with his right hand. "I just wish we knew what to call them."

They hadn't gone very far, when the Puns stopped. In front, there stood that large Human hut. David stood dumbfounded. Why were they here? Realizing the others were affrighted, he tried to give encouragement. "I don't think we have to worry with these creatures by our side. I wonder if this is where they live?"

One of the Puns gave out a loud sound. "Woof, woof." The sound was not like the Krogs high-pitched sound. It wasn't even like the growling sounds. He did it again. "Woof, woof." They heard the same grinding sound and a loud bang on the ground. At that, the Puns started to run toward the castle. David, Catrin, Griffin, and Meghan stood and watched, until a Pun came back and nudged Catrin with its head. "I get the point," Catrin laughed. "We're coming."

As they approached, Griffin inspected the cause of the loud bang. "Look at this. It's some kind of a giant door. See the chains. They must wind it up and down."

"Wow!" Meghan said in amazement. "Look at this thing. What a gigantic place. The Humans must have been giants."

"Yes, they are." Catrin answered. "My Pa said they can be about six feet tall."

David followed cautiously. It was a trait of any high prince or future high prince. When they stepped into the large Hall, he thought he was in a dream. On the walls were gold bowls with flames burning that gave light to the whole interior. The inside was beautiful with gold sculptures, elegant wall hangings, and portraits, large tables and chairs carved with strange designs, and large silver plates and bowls. In front of each large table were smaller replicas and Din-size plates and bowls. It was evident that Humans and Dins were comrades. Never had he seen such sights. At the head table, on a pedestal, was a mammoth book that was old and slightly tattered. He climbed onto a stool and opened the book carefully. It was written in English, the language of the Elfdins. He was amazed, as he scanned the pages with care. "Wait a minute." He looked down at Griffin. "Griffin, come up here. Look at this. I've found the name of these creatures. They're called Pundles, now we know what a carved Pundle must look like. They're called Puns for short and they're the companions of the Humans and Dins. And this place is called a castle." He laughed with glee. "It's all here in this book. This castle was owned by a Human called *Old Chronicler.*"

Meghan was studying the portraits on the walls. "It's all in these pictures. There's Puns, Dins, and the giants must be Humans. They resemble us, without pointed ears, and they all have different color hair like us. Catrin, David, Griffin, look at this one. What is that thing? It looks like it might be another place where Humans live."

"Griffin," David said. "I have a picture of the Gold Temple. There's Humans dressed like great prophet."

Catrin had gone to join Meghan to see the picture when David described the Gold Temple. "I believe that's what we're looking at here," Catrin said. "It's a magnificent hut with giants with robes like great prophet. There's also Dins dressed like him. All around them are Dins in our green garments, Humans dressed in strange clothes, and Pundles. It must be the Gold Temple in the Golden Age of Oralee. How I wish, we could return to those days."

After they had eaten, David decided they'd better head out. They couldn't afford to waste time. Their mission was to go to the Gold Temple. "We'll have to do double-time to make up for the time lost. The only question is how to get out of this place. Maybe if we go to the door, the Puns will show us." They all walked to the door and watched the Puns. One of them went over to what looked like a huge wooden wheel and stood inside one of the stalls. Four others joined him, and all pushed the wheel. As it turned, the loud grinding noise of the chain started. The giant door was lowered until it hit the ground.

David watched to see what the Puns would do, as they started to leave. He didn't have to wonder long. Several Puns were right behind them. "It seems they aren't going to let us get out of their sight. I believe they're going to follow." David folded his arms and laughed. "That's fine with me; I believe we'll all be much safer with them. At least we know that we aren't their enemy."

Chapter 8

The Gold Temple

"MY HIGH PRINCE!" DYLAN exclaimed, as he pointed across the water. "Look at that giant gold structure! Even with this shroud, it appears to be magnificent. How can anyone, even Humans, make something that colossal?"

The Crusaders all looked in the direction where Dylan pointed. With wide-eyed wonder, all but Drew gazed in awe. Somewhat in shock, he managed to speak. "My high prince, I believe that's the Gold Temple. I'm sure that's what it is."

Rhonda fidgeted with her left earlobe. "We've discovered it, but how do we journey across the water?"

Patrick stared. He was stunned at the wondrous sight of the Gold Temple. Then again, even some Humans would gaze in awe at seeing something resembling a giant gold Cathedral for the first time. Here at the end of Oralee was such a majestic edifice. But between the Dins and it was a massive river. If the Israelites thought that they'd hit a blockade, when faced with the Jordan, it was a lake compared to what this river seemed to the Dins. Patrick sighed heavily. "I don't know how we're going to get to the Gold Temple, unless there's a bridge or something.It's too dangerous to split up, so it looks like we'll have to go in one direction. If there's nothing to the right, we'll backtrack to the left. I know it's going to consume time, but we haven't an alternative. Between the Krogs and those giant creatures, we have to stay together."

It was a rocky walk along the riverbank, and travel for the Crusaders was slow. Patrick knew they were losing time, valuable time needed to get to the Gold Temple. Why did the ballad say a fortnight, when they had already traveled two extra days trying to cross the river? Patrick tried to keep the rest in good spirits, but he knew they were becoming discouraged. "We can't give up. There has to be a way across. Maybe we can't get there at the moment, but we know it exists. There must be a way across that we can't see. The ballad has been true to travel time. We were standing across from it, the morning of the fourteenth day."

Archer interrupted. "What's that sound?"

All were silent. Fletcher whispered to Patrick. "It's coming from behind us. We have to find a place to hide. It must be Krogs."

Patrick immediately took control of the situation. "It's Krogs alright. I can hear them communicating to one another. Everyone hurry! Let's hide underneath that huge rock. We'll climb under, and hope they don't know we're here."

Griffin was in awe as he stood at the riverbank and saw the Gold Temple. He felt the cry of his ancestors to worship there. Never had he sensed such spiritual awareness. "David," he said, clasping his hands, "there's something awesome about that place. I believe the Sovereign God lives there, or visits there. It's something that I can't put my finger on. My heart yearns to be in there."

David and Meghan glared wide eyed. Catrin wiped tears from her eyes. "Griffin, I know what you mean. I can't explain what's happening to me. My heart is so full of joy that I have to cry."

David noticed the Puns were restless. One of them started to walk along the riverbank and several others followed. "Hey, Catrin, Griffin, Meghan, I don't know what the Puns are doing, but we better follow. I believe that they are sensing something. Whatever it is, I believe we're safer with them than standing here by ourselves."

All four followed close by the Puns. It was difficult to keep up with the rocky terrain, but they were young and in shape. Suddenly, the Puns stopped. Two of them stood on each side of the Dins, two more in back and two others in front. Catrin laughed. "I do believe that they're escorting us."

Griffin scratched the back of his head with his right hand. "I think we're being protected. They are clever creatures."

Meghan noticed Puns sniffing the air as they walked. Off in the distance, she thought she saw Krogs. "Puns are mazers for sure. I believe there's an army of Krogs ahead. Puns do sniff like Krogs. All the time we were trying to avoid them, they were protecting us. They know the difference between the scent of Dins and Krogs. I don't know how they do. Dins haven't seen a Pun for generations. It must be a natural instinct."

David was sure that he heard Krogs attacking in the distance. "I don't want to alarm you all, but that sound is Krogs attacking." He pointed to the army of Krogs ahead of them. "That army is heading in that direction."

Griffin patted his lips with his right forefinger. "Whatever they're fighting, it can't be Puns. I don't hear any sounds of Puns."

Catrin pointed to the Puns. "Why aren't they moving ahead? Why are they just standing here? Surely, they have to know that Krogs are fighting something."

David rubbed the back of his neck with his right hand. "I'm sure if it was Dins, they would look to protect them. This is most strange. Is there something else in Oralee more powerful than Puns?"

The Crusaders had found a cave under the rock and made a barricade of rocks and branches at the entrance. Krogs marched closer, a horde of beasts ready for battle. Patrick motioned for the others to come closer and whispered. "They must know we're here. It's an army, not scouts. I believe they have our destruction in mind."

Fletcher gestured with his right hand. "My high prince, do you want Rhonda, Owen, and Kevyn to help me make more arrows?"

"Yes. If the four of you can keep us supplied with arrows, the beasts will have to go some to get at us. There may be a multitude of the beasts, but they can only get through the cleft a few at a time. After a while, they'll have to pull the dead carcasses out of their way."

Drew gathered dry branches and grass and piled them near the barricade before he spoke to Patrick. "I've made preparation for a flame. If it gets too tough, we could always light the flame. Krogs are more affrighted of that than the other creatures. They attack the creatures, but they've never tried to fight the Sacred Flame that guards the tunnel entrance."

"I don't think a flame would be too wise here. How will we breathe with all that smoke?"

Drew put both hands on his head. "I think I'm quite addled. What was I thinking? I'm glad that one of us thinking clearly."

Dylan grabbed Patrick's arm, gasped at what he'd done, then bowed his head. "My high prince, I believe the beasts are in combat."

Patrick motioned for all to be quiet. He patted Dylan on the back. "I believe that you're right. I hear their squealing cries of pain."

"But what are they fighting?" Kevyn said. "I don't hear anything else."

Rhonda fidgeted her left earlobe. "Perhaps it's superlative that we don't know,"

"Precisely my conclusion," Owen responded.

Archer hurried to look out a hole in the branches. "I can't see them; they're too far away.How come we can't hear anything else? What are they fighting?" He rubbed his forehead with his right hand. "I don't believe that they would be attacking each other. It doesn't make any sense. Why can't we hear anything but them squealing?"

Patrick listened with his eyebrows squished together and shook his head. "I'm addled. It doesn't make a bit of sense. If it was the growling creatures, we'd hear them. Let's move the limb against this side. I'll creep out and check things out." He squeezed through the opening and stood near the side of the cleft. But he was back inside and bracing the beam within seconds. "There's another army heading in our direction. It's bigger than I've ever seen."

Owen gestured with both hands. "My high prince, what are they combating? Did you observe?"

"I didn't have a chance. When I saw the other army, I didn't give them time to spot me. They must be coming to help the ones screeching. Maybe when they go by, I can take another look."

Catrin was addled that they could hear that the Krogs were in battle in the distance, but they heard no other sound except the beasts in pain. She observed David and knew he was just as addled. "You can't figure out what they're fighting either, can you? The beasts are screeching from agony, but no other sounds are heard. What are they fighting? It can't be Puns, because I don't hear any growls."

As she spoke, Griffin and Meghan listened.

Griffin tapped his lips with his right forefinger. "I know what you mean. I was questioning the same thing. If it was Dins, we would hear their screaming. Besides, the Puns would help, but they're just sitting here. I'm addled; it doesn't make a bit of sense. Maybe we should go and make sure it's not the Crusaders. I know Puns have protected us, but perhaps they haven't seen the others."

Catrin twirled her black hair around her right forefinger. "I don't believe the Puns have to see Dins; I believe they smell them."

Meghan stood with a determined look. "I can't take this any longer. If it's the Crusaders, the Puns can help them. I may be overly cautious, but that's my Pa out there," she said twisting her hands. She took a deep breath. "Let's go."

They all nodded in the affirmative and started to walk toward the battle, but Puns grabbed them by their backside and pulled them back. "Ouch!" Catrin yelled. "You're biting me. Stop that. It hurts."

David gestured with his right hand. "Listen to me. They obviously don't want us to leave. We'd better move back to where we were and sit down."

Griffin folded his arms and laughed. "They're determined to keep us here. "Catrin said they were mazers; she wasn't joking."

Meghan twisted her hands and looked down. "But what if it is the Crusaders? Shouldn't we do something?"

Catrin threw up her hands. "I believe if they were there, the Puns would know. After all, they knew where we were every time we were in trouble with Krogs."

Griffin nodded his head. "I agree with Catrin. If it was the Crusaders, I believe that the Puns would have done something."

David sat and watched the Puns. He knew something was brewing, but he didn't understand them. What were they waiting for? Where were the Crusaders? How would they get to the Gold Temple? Were there any Humans left? Before he knew what was happening, the Puns nudged them all in the opposite direction from the battle. Catrin went to stop, but a nudge to her backside kept her moving. She ran to catch up with David. "What's going on? Do you have any idea where they're taking us?"

He noticed some high rocks with clefts ahead. "I think they want to hide us." David pointed up toward the rocks. "Look ahead. I believe they want to conceal us in those rocks."

Climbing as quickly as possible, they slipped into one of the clefts, while the Puns sat on rocks below. David perused where they had come from. Krogs by the thousands were heading toward the battle. "Look at the beasts. I had no idea there were that many in Oralee." He noticed the Puns slouching flat on the rocks and pointed to them. "I think they're hiding. They know that there's too many for them to fight and protect us at the same time."

Griffin felt that sensation to be in the Gold Temple worshiping like his ancestors. The call was strong, but he said nothing. Yet, at the same time, Catrin started to cry. "I have to get to the Gold Temple; I'm almost overwhelmed by this strong feeling to be there."

Griffin went to respond, but noticed the Puns were up. One gazed up at David and started to walk away. He got the hint. "Okay, warriors, they want us to follow."

Meghan shuddered and stood up. "Where are they taking us? We seem to be safe here."

Catrin threw her arms in the air. "I don't understand this. Now, they have us heading toward the battle. They stopped us earlier. There are too many Krogs. We have no chance against that many. What are they doing?"

David heard heavy thumps coming toward them, but the Puns weren't alarmed. He went to say something, but Griffin spoke first. "I think more Pundles are coming."

Catrin turned to her right and stood with her hands on her hips. "Look at all those Puns. There has to be thousands. Where'd they come from? No wonder we've been waiting. These Puns boggle my mind; I've never seen such mazers. I just adore them."

The Pundle army went ahead of them. Some of the Puns guarding the Dins joined the army, while others took their places as guards. David was amazed at their strategic maneuvers. "I don't know what's ahead, but I believe they have everything in control."

Chapter 9

The Armies Gather

PATRICK WENT TO TAKE another survey, but again, found himself back before he could see what the Krogs were fighting. "It's an army of the beasts, bigger than any of us could imagine. I didn't realize how many there were. I'm addled. How did we get past them? Where are they coming from? Why haven't we seen that many before? We better sit still. If they find us, we'll be history."

With the multitude of Krogs on the march, the ground shook near the cave. The Crusaders felt the earth move. Patrick was determined to keep them calm. "Don't worry; we'll be fine. We're just going to have to wait till they're past, then we'll head out of here." He heard a crashing noise and beheld Archer being buried under the load. He ran to him calling the others to help. "We have to get him out."

They all stopped short; the side was caving in. Somewhat dazed, they stood in confusion.Falconer broke the silence. "It's no use; we'll be buried with him. We can't get to him."

Patrick snapped out of his shock. "Follow me to the end of the cave. There's a turn with an opening, wide enough for us to stay in. We'll have to see about digging out after this is over. There's no time to lose. We have to get deeper inside before more caves in." Everyone jumped at the sound of another crash; the barricade was falling in. "Run!" Patrick yelled, grabbing Rhonda by the arm. "Hurry or we'll be crushed." Drew stood still and starred. Patrick seized Drew's arm with his other hand and pulled hard. "Come on. We can't lose you too."

Huddled together in a spirit of forlornness, they couldn't believe Archer was gone. They had come so far and to lose one now was boggling. After a long span of silence, it was Gwent who finally spoke. "My high prince, what can we do? I suppose we're buried in. How will we ever get out?"

Patrick stood still and traced the scar from his right temple to his cheek with his fingers, "I'm afraid that at this time, I've no answers. First, we have to wait till we hear no beasts marching. The ground is still trembling from their armies. How we'll get out is beyond me. I'm too addled to think of anything helpful. Give me time to get my bearings. We're all affrighted about the situation." Putting his right hand on Drew's left shoulder, Patrick gazed into his eyes. "Are you all right? Words seem futile. What can I say?"

Drew's head hung as he bit his bottom lip. "I don't know what to think. How am I going to tell Vanora? My poor lass is carrying their first bairn. They've been so excited; that's all they talk about." He threw up his hands. "How will I tell her?" He paused and looked Patrick in the eyes. "But then again, we're probably all doomed. We can't survive in here for long without air. Maybe it was better for Archer to go quickly."

Pundles were keeping close to the Dins. David wasn't sure if they were being too protective, but he didn't really care if they were. He kept surveying the area, when he noticed Griffin seemed dazed. Before he could ask what was wrong, Griffin pointed his finger toward the Gold Temple. "Krogs are on the other side of the river. I don't remember seeing them before. Where'd they come from? They're headed for the Gold Temple."

"Look!" Catrin said. "The beasts are walking on the water; they're crossing. How are they doing that? But what in Oralee is that black figure? It looks like a Din, but it seems different."

David watched the figure in the distance that forced the Krogs into the water. "Whatever he is, he's making the beasts enter the water. If they don't, he points that oak shillelagh at them. He's causing them to shriek with pain."

Catrin placed her hands on her hip and laughed. "They're not in battle. No wonder we couldn't hear anything else. It's that Din like creature's cane that's stinging them or something."

Meghan grasped David's arm and pointed. "What's to your right? Why are those Krogs near that huge rock in the distance? What are they after? It looks like they're trying to dig at something."

Griffin stood on a nearby rock to get a better look. "If I was them, I'd be trying to hide from that dark figure."

David laughed. "They won't get far. Look at the Puns darting in their direction; they look mad." He lost his grin and his eyebrows scrunched together. "Wait a minute. There's something strange going on. They haven't gone after the beasts yet. Why have they changed their tactics? They've been avoiding the Krogs up-to-now. Maybe it's crazy, but I think it's the Crusaders."

It was only a matter of minutes, and the beasts were dashing from the rock. As soon as the coast was clear, David, Griffin, Catrin, and Meghan ran to the rock with Pun guards by their side. To their amazement, it was a cave entrance. Some of the Puns were digging away. David decided there was only one way to find out if the cave held the Crusaders; he'd blow the war horn just loud enough for anyone in the cave to hear. "I'll blow the horn; and we'll listen for an answer." He blew quickly and listened quietly, but heard no response. Feeling compelled to try again, he blew once more. Immediately, Patrick's horn answered.

Inside the cave, the Crusaders had almost given up hope. At the sound of David's war horn, Patrick thought he dreamed it. When it sounded again, he knew it was real and at once answered.

Drew blamed himself for Archer's death. If he had only called on the Sovereign God, he might be alive. He didn't want to take any chances with the rest of them. He no sooner called out for help, and he heard the war horn. When he heard the horn, he was elated. "My high prince, I do believe that we're going to be rescued.

The Sovereign God heard me. He must have chased the beasts away. I don't hear them at the entrance anymore."

Patrick gestured with his right hand. "I know it was David's horn. I don't know how I heard it here; he's in the colony. All I know is that something is dragging branches, moving rocks, and digging through."

"Outside the cave, the four young warriors all pulled stones and dug earth to clear the entrance. Meghan went to step forward and heard a sound. She stepped back and moved carefully. "I believe someone is caught under here. There's a moaning noise. It will take all of us to move this large timber out of our way."

Unable to move the log, David had an idea. "Let's tie a rope around it, and let the Puns pull it. Griffin and I will guide it over whoever is under there, while you two see if you can help pull him out."

The beam moved slowly. Meghan was on her knees digging away the dirt, when she noticed a trench under the beam. "He's down in here. It looks like he's been protected in this trench." She motioned to Catrin. "Hurry! I need help to pull him out." Catrin joined her and they gently pulled him out. Meghan became dizzy, when she saw his face. "It's Archer. I think he's breathing." She grabbed her head with both hands. "He has to be. My sister and he have so many plans for the bairn. He just has to be alive."

Archer moaned and opened his eyes. "Where am I?" He shook his head. "Meghan, is that you?"

Meghan and Catrin cried. David helped him to his feet and laughed. "Yes, it's Meghan.And to answer where you are, you are part of the Crusaders on your way to the Gold Temple. Are the others under there with you?"

"I don't know where they are. All I remember is hearing a noise before you pulled me out. I must have been knocked out. The others have to be in there. We'd better get them out."

Once Patrick realized there were others outside digging them out, he and the Crusaders stood back from the debris. It was Drew that first saw a glimmer of light. "They're almost through; I see light and air is flowing in."

Patrick saw the giant creatures, grabbed his bow, and yelled to the others. "Set your bows. The giant creatures are digging through."

"Don't shoot!" David screamed. "They are not an enemy. Pa, please don't shoot any of them. They're here to help you."

Patrick and the rest lowered their bows and froze in their place as they saw Archer squeeze through the opening. Drew grabbed him, fell on his neck and hugged him. "My lad, I thought you were dead. This is a glorious day."

Griffin came through next and motioned for them to follow him. "Let's get out of here. I don't want a cave in or something. We better talk outside."

Once they were safely outside, Prince Patrick glared at his lad. He didn't know whether to discipline or applaud him. "What are you doing out of the colony? Who's in charge of the Dins? Who's leading them?" He paused as he saw Catrin. And mercy me, what in Oralee is your sister doing with you? I don't know what I am going to do with you three. First, Rhonda shoots a Krog that almost had me in its clutches, and now you two save all of us." He rubbed his temple with his right hand. "But how in Oralee did you get those creatures to help you?"

Drew shook his head and looked at Griffin and Meghan. "Griffin, what are you doing here? Meghan, are you all right?"

Griffin laughed. "We followed David and Catrin. Meghan told me that she had an impression or something and she believed that she had to come. Come to find out, David said that he had the same notion."

Catrin ran to hug Rhonda and they both cried. Once Catrin composed herself, she placed her hands on her hips and exclaimed. "Really! Rhonda! As if Ma didn't have enough to be affrighted about with Pa leading the Crusaders, you go and pull some fool crazy move."

Rhonda looked down at her feet. "I should have informed you. It wasn't a dream, because I was awake. But I thought you might think I was addled."

Catrin threw her hands up in the air. "What in Oralee are you talking about?"

"I was told that as the next spiritual mentor, I had to join the Crusaders to be at the Gold Temple when the Humans arrive."

Patrick folded his arms. "Who told you to join the Crusaders?"

"It was a bright light that told me to go."

"Wow!" David exclaimed. "It had to be the Sovereign God." He gestured towards Catrin with his right hand. "He told Catrin that we were supposed to come. Of course, I already had the impression that we had to do something." He laughed and turned to the prince. "Pa, these aren't creatures; they're Pundles. Remember, the ballad said carved Pundle? Well, now we know what a Pundle is. They've been protecting us since we reached the end of the Great Forest. They took us inside one of the Human huts that are called castles. An old book revealed that it belonged to a Human called *Old Chronicler*. I read the book and that's how we found out their names. Furthermore, we also found out that they are companions of Humans and Elfdins."

"David, we're wasting time." Griffin interrupted. "We have to get to the Gold Temple. The beasts have crossed the river. I don't know what that black figure is, but it's on the other side with them."

Patrick stared across the river. "How did they get across? I don't see any bridge."

"They walked on the water," Catrin said. "We saw them."

Meghan had run ahead to the spot where the Krogs crossed. She went close to the edge. "David! Come here. Look at this. Bless me; it's a bridge that's hidden under the water. You can't see it unless you're at it. The Krogs crossed by walking on the bridge."

David starred in wonder. He couldn't believe his eyes. "Pa! There is a bridge. Why is it hidden in the water? How did that black figure know it was here?"

Patrick realized he'd heard them mention a black figure that wasn't a Krog. "What black figure? You forget we were hindered during their crossing."

Catrin gestured with both hands. "We don't know. We thought it was a Din, but it almost resembles the beasts. It's really evil looking."

"Yes," said Griffin, scratching the back of his head. "We saw it standing near the edge of the river and piercing the beasts to make them cross. From a distance, we thought they were in battle. He used an oak shillelagh to make them jump into the water. When he pointed it at them, they squealed in pain and jumped in."

Patrick shook his head, folded his arms, and looked at Catrin. "What do you mean, the Sovereign God told you to come?" Before she could answer, he turned to Rhonda. "And you, my lass, have some answering to do. You never told us you were told to come."

Rhonda felt her face flush. "Sorry, I contemplated that you might consider me more addled than Catrin would and that's why I didn't say anything. It was rather an extraordinary episode."

David rubbed the back of his neck with his right hand. "Catrin dreamed while she was waiting for me to come back from the hunt. When I got back, she said the Sovereign God had spoken to her and said, 'you and David are my warriors, and I want you to travel to the Gold Temple. You must not tarry a moment.' When he spoke, Catrin said it was a beautiful white light, bright, and warm."

Drew was thrilled as he listened. "That's what I've heard about the Sovereign God." He then turned towards Rhonda. "But I also heard that He is a bright light. The two of you must have heard from him. What wonderful encounters; the Sovereign God spoke to them." He threw up his arms. "Catrin's not even the great prophetess nor is Rhonda the spiritual mentor; this is most boggling. I must talk to them." He hurried over to where they stood. "You both must tell me the whole story from top to bottom. I must hear it all."

Patrick gestured with both hands. "All right, while they are explaining to you, we're all going to cross this river." He touched David's right arm. "Do you think the Pundles will come?"

David laughed as he looked at the river's edge. "They seem to read our minds. Look at the Puns take to the water." He then placed his right hand on his Patrick's left shoulder. "Pa. It's easier if you call them Puns; the book said it's their nickname."

Chapter 10

The Revelation

Evil Druxin hurried the Krogs to the Gold Temple. "Move it! I can't let the Dins get in there." He hit the nearest Krogs with a bolt from his oak shillelagh and grumbled to himself. "Someone has contacted the Sovereign God. That's the only way the Great Doors could have opened without black power."

Raven and the other elders hurried their groups to meet up with Evil. As soon as Evil saw them, he conversed with the elders to bring them up-to-date. "We must prevent the Dins from turning the light of the Gold Cross with the inscription of the Sovereign God toward Oralee." Then he continued to hurry his assembly along. "You dirty beasts best hurry, if you know what's good for you. I've worked too many years to destroy Oralee's belief in the Sovereign God. I'll not be stopped now. I'll defeat him once-and-for-all. He'll not have his way this time." Evil shook his fist toward heaven, and then he turned and unleashed a few lightning bolts at the Krogs nearest him. "I told you to move it. I gave no order to dawdle."

Raven was by his side now and the veins in Evil's forehead were enlarged as he spoke. "It's entirely his fault. He'll be the God of nothing when I finish." Almost tripping over a Krog in front of him, Evil Druxin struck the creature with a double bolt that almost killed it. "He's always had favorites. But I kept his other pets on Gold Mountain, until all Dins forgot about him. This time I'll be great prophet. My power has grown since our last encounter. Besides, I have enough Krogs to annihilate every Din in Oralee that tries to fight us. One thing about these beasts, they do multiply quickly," he said with an evil chortle.

Trying to rush the Krogs along, Evil Druxin didn't notice the door to the Gold Temple was closed. The puns had run around the Krog army and secured the door. He was beside himself when he noticed it. Taking a tantrum, he started to hit any Krog in his reach. "I'll get my revenge on the Sovereign God for choosing my brother as great prophet. His descendants are still the spiritual leaders, but that will soon end."

Evil Druxin tried desperately to break in the door, but his power wouldn't penetrate it. Maybe he'd have to resort to physical means. "You mangy beasts find me a beam. If we don't get in there before any Dins do, we're all doomed. My power to keep us alive in Oralee will be destroyed if that Gold Cross shines its light toward Oralee. I will not lose; I've come too far."

The Puns kept the Dins hidden within their army as they moved along the outer edge of the temple grounds. Evil was so busy with the door that he didn't notice the maneuver. Patrick and the rest were astonished at the size of the Gold Temple. "I'm boggled," Patrick said. "This place is magnificent. But why are the Puns taking us around to the back side?"

David shook his head and smiled. "I know one thing for sure, these Puns are clever. They know something that we don't. That has boggled us from the first. It's as if someone is giving them orders or something. I can't explain it, but we have learned that we let them lead and we follow."

Catrin nodded her head. "That's right. We let them lead and we follow."

"Look!" Griffin said. "They've brought us to a cave."

Before any of the others could respond, the Puns were nudging them all to enter. It didn't take them too long to figure out what they were supposed to do. Patrick took command. "Let's see where this thing leads. It does seem that they know what they're doing. I guess wisdom lets them lead and we follow."

Patrick stopped suddenly, and Drew almost walked into him. "What are you stopping for?" Patrick pointed to his left. "The Puns are heading that way. It looks like a tunnel."

The Puns led them through the tunnel, until they stood at a huge door. One of the Puns made a growling noise, and movement was heard on the other side of the door. Before any of the Dins could figure out what was happening, a couple of the Puns pushed the door open. Patrick and the others found themselves entering into a majestic edifice. Like the castle in the Gold Valley, all the walls had gold bowls with flames that lightened everything. Never had they seen or dreamt of anything so splendid. The brilliance of color seemed to dazzle. Along the walls leading to the altar were carved figures set on pedestals. On the right were larger figurines of Humans. The left was lined with smaller carvings of Elfdins.

Unknown to the Dins was Human architecture. They stood in the midst of a Gold Temple that expressed High Gothic architectural principles. The skeletal structure of columns and arches soared to a hundred-foot vault. Framed in the arches were large stained-glass windows of golden yellow, brilliant ruby red, and sapphire blue. At the altar area were smaller windows of only golden yellow below the multi-colored ones. Under the gold windows was a beautifully carved archway shaped like a cross. The inside of the cross archway was lined with gold. The Dins were amazed to see all the gold objects resembling the ones on Gold Mountain; but they did not know what they were called.

Catrin with hands on her hips was the first to speak about the gold objects. "Does anyone know what those gold objects that resemble the large ones on Gold Mountain are called?"

Everyone shook their heads.

By this time, they were all gaping wide-eyed at the sight of the giant Gold Cross on the altar inside the archway. Before they knew what happened, Evil broke through with Krogs surging ahead of him. Dylan was the first to see them. "Krogs!" He shrieked readying his bow. Archer, Falconer, Fletcher, and Gwent set their arrows and ran to meet the onslaught of Krogs, with the squires close behind. David, Catrin, and Meghan followed suit. Arrow after arrow hit the screeching Krogs, but it was the Puns that rallied to the forefront to protect the Dins. It was a horrendous battle of Krogs being defeated. David realized they might hit a Pun by mistake and took the necessary precautions. He ran toward the stairs that lead to the balcony. "Follow me. We'll have a clear view from up there." Catrin, Archer, Dylan, Falconer, Fletcher, Rhonda, Owen, Meghan, Kevyn, and Gwent seeing that the Puns were in their way of fire followed David up the stairs to the balcony to get a clear aim at the Krogs.

Patrick, Drew, and Griffin were closest to the altar area, when Griffin spotted the carved Pundle. "Look he shouted, there's the carved Pundle."

Catrin hearing Griffin, turned her attention to the altar. She saw Evil channel a bolt of lightning through his oak shillelagh toward Patrick and Drew. "No!" She screamed and without any thought, she pointed her hand at the bolt. Out of her hand shot a bolt so strong that it stopped Evil's.

Evil Druxin shook his head in shock, but immediately turned his attention to Griffin. "Don't touch that or you'll die," he threatened as Griffin was about to touch the carved Pundle. "Get away from it now. One wave of my oak shillelagh will finish you off. I have the controlling power in here." At that moment, one of the Puns jumped on Evil from behind pushing him down. Evil Druxin immediately sent a ball of fire toward Griffin who stood near the carved Pundle. Before Griffin realized what he was doing, he put his right hand forward and dispelled the fire. Evil was furious. "How did you do that? You can't know anything about supernatural power." He unleashed lightning toward Griffin who sent a bolt toward Druxin. As soon as Evil's bolt hit Griffin's, it fizzled like water on fire. Griffin, aware that an unknown power was surging through him, sent a ball of fire that knocked Evil down. Druxin was so shocked that he couldn't think. Griffin took advantage of the moment and touched the carved Pundle and immediately the giant Gold Cross turned, and a bright light overtook the light of the flames on the walls. Eyes widened as they felt the warmth of the light.

Catrin turned to look at Evil. She watched his eyes dart frantically from Krog to Krog as they fell dead. When Evil looked at her, she shrieked. "What's happening? Who is killing the Krogs? They just seem to be dropping down dead."

While this was going on, Patrick noticed that the Humans were standing at the Portal. "We have to greet them." He shouted.

Drew almost got zapped with a bolt from Evil's oak shillelagh as he ran toward the Portal to welcome the Humans. But when he put his right hand toward it, Evil's bolt fizzled out. "C-come in," Drew said. "Come in. You must be the Humans."

Old Chronicler, the oldest Human alive with permission to enter Oralee, was the first to enter through the Portal. When he stepped forward, Evil sent a bolt that would have killed Old, but Rhonda saw it, and with both hands sent two bolts that sizzled out Evil's. At that, Evil was livid and sent a bolt towards Rhonda. Owen saw the bolt heading for Rhonda and with both hands sent two bolts that fizzled out Evil's.

Close behind were Godric the great prophet of the Humans and his wife, Great Prophetess Edith, Lord Archibald and Lady Catherine, Lord Eldrid and Lady Audrey, Duke Wilbur and Duchess Bernia, High Prince Ordway and High Princess Ardith, Sir Anthony Rice and Lady Roselee, Sir Richard Oswald and Lady Dawn, etc. All had to stand to the left of Old Chronicler who stood transfixed as his eyes darted around the Temple. Krogs fell dead without arrows or Puns. Old Chronicler's peripheral vision caught sight of some figures crawling out the Portal. "Stop him!" He yelled. But it was too late. Before anyone could do a thing, Evil, Raven, Carbon, Nightshade, and Soot were through the Portal into the Human world.

"Infernal!" Old Chronicler said as he punched the air. He sighed and shook his head. "That weasel got away. I should've

THE ELFDINS AND THE GOLD TEMPLE

known Druxin would be here. If we would have been on top of things, we'd have made precautions before we went through the Portal." He shook both fists and clenched his teeth. "Infernal! Infernal! Infernal!"

Griffin gazed at Old Chronicler in confusion. "What is going on? What are you talking about?"

Old Chronicler's lips vibrated as he blew out air. "We'd heard rumors that an evil prophet named Maddock was trying to get into Oralee through the Portal. While we were here, my young nephew, Squire Richard Oswald was found bound and gagged." He gestured towards his nephew. "He has since been knighted and has his gold cross back. "Anyway, one of his peers had found him. However, he couldn't say how he was bound, because the other young man knew nothing of Oralee. Maddock had stolen his gold cross, and he had no way of getting in to tell us." He punched his left hand with his right fist. "We all stayed for a few years longer last time. There had been war in our world, and we needed a long, peaceful rest. Oralee was a calm sea that we all desperately needed." He put his hands on his hips. "Having stayed so long, we were finally eager to return." He blew out air. "Instead of being so anxious to get back for our Great Harvest celebration, we should have paid more attention to the rumor. But who thought evil would get into Oralee? Besides, how could we know that Maddock had transformed himself into my nephew? No wonder he was so friendly to Druxin."

As Rhonda came near the crowd, Old Chronicler reached out and gave her a big hug. "I don't know who you are, but my appreciation cannot be overstated. Young lady, I'm called *Old Chronicler,* and I owe you my life."

"How did I do that?" Rhonda asked, fidgeting her left earlobe. "That must be why the bright light, I mean the Sovereign God, told me to be present when the Humans arrived."

"All Elfdins have supernatural power," Old Chronicler laughed. However, it is obvious by your ash blond hair and gray eyes that you are a spiritual mentor. Only the great prophet and great prophetess are more powerful than the spiritual mentors and following them are the high prince and high princess. Simply put, the tallest have the greatest abilities and down the line." He sat down on a bench. "What am I saying, you should know that." He placed his right hand on top of his head. "I think that near death incident has me all flustered. All I can say is thank the Sovereign God for having you here."

Rhonda saw Owen come forward and gave him a hug. "I do declare that you saved my life."

Owen laughed. "I consider that was the phenomenal power that I said I would use."

David stared at Old Chronicler with a questioning look. "But no Human has been here for over four hundred years. If you're Old Chronicler, how can you be alive? We were in your hut, I mean your castle." He rubbed the back of his neck with his right hand. "All the Dins of that day have been dead a long time."

Old Chronicler laughed. "Lordy me, young prince! Don't you remember the time difference between the two worlds?"

David shook his head. "We don't know anything about any time difference." He gestured towards Drew with his right hand. "Did you know that there is a time difference?"

Drew hung his head. "We have no records of the time when Humans visited us." He shrugged his shoulders. "To be honest, we weren't even sure if Humans still existed."

Old Chronicler clapped his hands together and chuckled. "I assure you that we exist. But the time difference is simple to explain. He sat back and folded his arms. "If we remain in Oralee for twenty-four days, when we return to our world, we've only aged a day."

"Wow!" Owen said. "You mean that twenty-four hours to Humans is twenty-four days to us?"

Old Chronicler threw back his head and let out a peal of laughter. "You've got it, young spiritual mentor."

Catrin threw her right fist up in the air. "That's what it meant to greet past Humans. It's Humans that were already here."

Patrick rubbed the scar from his right temple to his chin with his fingers and stared at the old man. "We've gone through about four hundred years, and it's only been about seventeen years in your world. That's a mazer."

"Excuse me!" Griffin said. "You said you should have known Druxin would be here. Who is he? We've never seen him before today."

Great Prophet Godric who stood beside Old Chronicler answered. "When we were here last, Druxin felt that he should have been great prophet and not his twin brother. As you know, the rule has always been the one who possessed all the physical requirements. Druxin blamed the Sovereign God and claimed He favored Arthur. There wasn't any favoritism. Arthur wanted to please his God. Druxin wanted to please himself. Sort of like Jacob and Esau in the Bible."

Griffin stood perplexed. "Bible, what is that?"

Old Chronicler scratched his head. "I do believe they have lived in the Dark Ages since we were here last. The Bible is the book that tells you all about the Sovereign God." He gave out a heavy sigh. "We have some serious educating to do."

Catrin gave a puzzled look. "I believe you are right, but as for Druxin, we were taught that Druxin had apologized to Arthur and soon after was one of the Krogs first victims."

Godric shook his head. "It must have been all part of his dark power. It seems evil was working to get into Oralee and Druxin was the one it chose."

"Yes," sighed Old Chronicler, "but he had to welcome it."

Godric nodded his head. "Quite true. Evil can't choose you, unless you choose it."

Patrick was the next to give a puzzled look. "How did the evil get in?"

"Like Old Chronicler said, it was an evil prophet named Maddock that bound and gagged his nephew, and he stole his nephew's gold cross to enter through the Portal. He transformed himself into Richard, and brought two black cats with him. Maddock trained Druxin in the ways of his god of evil until Druxin knew black power." He paused to look at Catrin who was staring with her eyebrows scrunched together.

She realized that he knew she wished to ask him something and smiled. "What are cats? You said he brought two of them, but we don't know what a cat is?"

Old Chronicler laughed. "Lordy me, young lady. But you've been fighting them for four hundred years. The black beasts that lay all around us are the results of those cats. You see, Oralee is a supernatural place. Normal cats from our world became huge ugly monsters in Oralee because of the spell Maddock cast on them."

Rhonda fidgeted with her left earlobe. "Excuse me, but if Sir Richard's gold cross was stolen, how did he acquire it back?"

Meghan twisted her hands. "That's what I was wondering."

Old Chronicler sat back and folded his arms. "We were all waiting for Maddock to come back through the Portal. His evil power was no contest against High Prophet Godric and High Prophetess Rowena." He then gestured towards Godric with his right hand. "He'll tell the rest of the story."

Godric nodded towards Old. "Once we had him caught, he gave a complete confession before we locked him away for life. It seems that he had Evil Druxin turn the Gold Cross around which prevented us from getting back into Oralee. It also meant since the words *Sovereign God* engraved on the cross no longer faced Oralee that his light no longer shined on Oralee; that's why the shroud covered the light of the sun. Evil wanted Oralee to be in perpetual darkness. The witch of Narnia made it always winter, Evil made it always foggy and gloomy; if he could have, he would have stopped daytime all together."

"I was fit to be tied when it finally occurred to us," Old Chronicler said, "that no one was going to turn the Gold Cross around."

Rhonda fidgeted her left earlobe. "I understand that those gold objects are crosses, but what do they signify?"

Old Chronicler shook his head. "We'll get into all that later. First, we have to start at the beginning."

High Prophetess Edith interjected. "After five of our years, we figured that we weren't getting back in."

"By that time," Godric said, "you had been fighting Krogs for over a century. From what I gather, it seems that Evil Druxin had caused Oralee to forget about the Sovereign God."

Drew was completely boggled. "I seem to have supernatural power; I'm totally addled. We haven't even seen our Sacred Books to find out how to get our supernatural power back."

Great Prophet Godric pointed to the Gold Cross. "Your supernatural power is not found in some book. It's the Sovereign God who gives you power through the laying on of the hands of the spiritual mentors. We had been praying outside the Portal for someone in Oralee to be sensitive to him." He gestured with his right hand. "You see, he could not restore your power until you recognized him as your God."

Dylan jumped up. "But I did lay my hands on all the Dins when they turned twelve, and naught happened."

Edith smiled. "Yes, but no one had yet recognized him as God."

Catrin's eyebrows scrunched together. "How can you pray to the Sovereign God of the Elfdins?"

Old Chronicler was beside himself with laughter. "Young lady, there is only one God of all creation."

Godric interjected. "The Sovereign God is the God who created Humans, Elfdins, Pundles, etc. He is the Creator of all there is."

"Right," Edith said. "There is nothing that exists that He did not create."

Rhonda fidgeted her left earlobe. "Are you declaring that He created the evil Krogs?"

Old grabbed his head with both hands. "He did not create evil; evil was created by the devil." He put up his hands. "Don't ask me who he is. All I can say is that we have to give you some Bible lessons."

Edith looked around. "I think that we have to find all the Sacred Books that were here. Everything is missing. Once we find them, we will have all the Bibles that we need to teach you all about the Sovereign God. If Druxin destroyed them, we'll just go back through the Portal and bring some back."

Catrin threw her hands up into the air. "I understand what happened. It seems that Druxin had Oralee so concerned with Krogs that everyone was convinced that they stole our supernatural power, but Oralee had forgotten the God of its power. Without the Sovereign God, there is no supernatural power."

"Amen!" Great Prophetess Edith exclaimed, clasping her hands. "I do perceive that you are next in line to be the great prophetess of the Elfdins with that revelation. Of course, your raven black hair and emerald eyes confirm it," she said with a laugh.

Catrin blushed at being acknowledged by this great and powerful lady.

David looked confused. "We had no idea there were so many Krogs. How come there were only a few that came into the Ravine? If they had all come in, they would have climbed Gold Mountain and destroyed us all."

Meghan twisted her hands. "Yes, we were amazed at the multitude that we encountered on our way here."

Godric pointed to the Gold Cross. "We had asked the Sovereign God to speak to the Pundles to watch over the Elfdins. Druxin hadn't counted on them remaining faithful. They kept thousands of Krogs out, but the Sovereign God told them to stay out. It was not for you to know of their existence until someone contacted him." He Paused at Catrin's doubtful stare. "You have a question?"

She hesitated, but answered anyway. "We didn't contact him; He came to me in a dream. I was thinking about him when my Pa told us about him dispelling evil, but I never spoke to him."

Before Godric could speak, Rhonda chimed in. "Yes, I didn't converse with him either; He communicated to me through a bright light."

"He heard both your hearts and answered. In fact, there were several of you calling on him from your heart. The fact that He moved proves that. Apparently, Druxin had kept a watch on the temple door, which would be the sign if contact with the Sovereign God had been made."

Griffin's eyebrows scrunched together. "But how would the temple door let Druxin know?"

"As long as it was closed, no contact had taken place. But once it opened, he must have moved to stop anyone from entering. He was so consumed by his evil power that he deceived himself into thinking that he would win against the Sovereign God."

Meghan's eyes widened. "Wow!"

"This is utterly unbelievable!" Owen exclaimed.

Catrin placed her hands on her hips. "But who opened the door?"

Dylan turned to Catrin. "That is precisely my inquiry."

Old Chronicler laughed, and leaned back in his seat. "The Sovereign God, of course."

"Until Maddock," Godric continued, "evil had never been in Oralee. Only the Humans that serve the Sovereign God are given the gold crosses that resemble the giant one at the Portal." He held up his cross with his right hand. "Without one of these, there is no entering Oralee. It had always been the only world without evil."

"Wait a minute!" Patrick said. "How did Druxin just get out? Certainly the Sovereign God didn't give him a gold cross."

Sir Richard Oswald clasped his hands. "Uncle, that's why we couldn't find Sir Reginald's gold cross when he died." He turned towards Patrick. "Sir Reginald was dying, but he wanted to die in Oralee. He had been badly wounded in the war, and he wanted to live his last days in our castle. You see, he didn't have a castle in our world. Anyway, he was my brother, and I couldn't find his gold cross when he died. We all looked high and low and it was nowhere to be found. I figured that he must have buried it, because he wouldn't need it anymore."

Rhonda fidgeted with her left earlobe. "But how could Druxin use your brother's gold cross to leave Oralee? Wouldn't the Sovereign God know that he is not Sir Reginald?"

Godric picked up his gold cross and held it up. "We only need the gold cross to get into Oralee; we don't need one to leave." He gestured towards Sir Richard. "He didn't mean that his brother's gold cross was needed for Druxin to leave. He realized that if

Druxin left, he must think that he has a way to return. Common sense says it's his brother's missing gold cross."

Griffin scratched the back of his head with his right hand. "How will we keep Druxin from getting back into Oralee?"

Old Chronicler gave out a loud laugh and shook his head. "Like I said we'll have a lot of instruction to do. For now, we'd all like to see the condition of our castles."

David folded his arms and laughed. "Well, we know that yours is in excellent condition; we had a Pundle tour."

At this time, High Prince Ordway and High Princess Heather joined them. Ordway spoke first. "Excuse me, but we really do have to move along. Our castle is the largest, and if it's in as good condition as Old Chronicler's, we can continue our conversation there."

Princess Heather smiled. "I do pray that it's in comparable condition. It's quite obvious that the Elfdins have a lot of knowledge to catch up on."

Great Prophet Drew laughed. "You'll have to lead the way. I'm afraid that we have no idea where your castle is."

Prince Ordway nodded his head. "Okay, let's go."

They all followed behind. It almost felt like a celebration of some kind. Catrin was the one who first spotted the castle. "Wow! That is almost as huge as the Gold Temple. We'll have no problem fitting in there."

Everyone waited outside while Prince Ordway and Princess Heather inspected their castle. They were both overjoyed as they toured the inside. "I should have known." High Prince Ordway chuckled. "The Sovereign God has not only had the Pundles guarding the castles, but I am sure that he has kept all of them whole."

Princess Heather raised both her hands. "Praise him! Except needing a little cleaning, everything seems to be fine."

As they went through Gold Valley, it was confirmed that the Sovereign God had protected all the Human castles; all were preserved. Outside of some minor wear and needing a bit of cleaning, they were completely fit for human habitation.

However, the Krogs and Evil had practically demolished all the Elfdin castles; they would need to be rebuilt. The only Din castle still standing was the Great Prophet's. It appeared that Druxin wanted that castle for himself. However, others were so destroyed that if the Humans had not known that a castle had been there, there was no trace that a building had ever existed. It was the Humans that informed the Dins where the High Prince and High Princess, the Spiritual Mentors, Archer, Falconer, Fletcher and other of the elders' castles had been located.

Epilogue

Oralee Restored

THE HUMANS AND THE Elfdins soon became bonded as in earlier times with the Humans thoroughly educating the Dins about the Sovereign God and the Cross. The hunger for knowledge was almost unquenchable. The Dins seemed to soak in everything like a sponge. They hungered to please and worship their God. With him back in his rightful place, the Sovereign God shone brightly on all endeavors. Joy and merriment returned as if it had never vanished.

With the help of the Humans, the Elfdins rebuilt their smaller castles in the Gold Valley in record time. All of which had grand entrances for the Pundles. It seems that the Puns and Dins became inseparable. The Golden Age returned with Drew, Meredith, Catrin, and Griffin being trained to lead in the worship of the Sovereign God at the Gold Temple.

Gone were the years of war and the need of weapons and defensive tactics. There was no more need of physical warfare. They were in right relationship with the Sovereign God who fully restored their supernatural powers; peace and prosperity reigned throughout all of Oralee.

It was with great anticipation that this generation of Elfdins observed their first Great Festival celebration on Gold Mountain. With a unanimous vote, Griffin and Catrin were chosen to lead them in worship to the Sovereign God, with David and Meghan by their side.

As Griffin and Catrin stretched their arms towards Heaven, David, Meghan, and all Elfdins followed suit and loudly sang: *"Sovereign God, we worship you. Sovereign God, we worship you. We worship you, our God. We worship you, our God!"*